THE HOUSE ON BOULBY CLIFF

Kevin Corby Bowyer

Mysterious Strawberry

Copyright © 2020 Kevin Corby Bowyer

All rights reserved

The characters and events portrayed in this book are fictitious. Any similarity to real persons, living or dead, is coincidental and not intended by the author.

No part of this book may be reproduced, or stored in a retrieval system, or transmitted in any form or by any means, electronic, mechanical, photocopying, recording, or otherwise, without express written permission of the publisher.

ISBN-13: 9798643419426

Cover design by: Joseph Loganbill

Printed in the United Kingdom

CONTENTS

Title Page — 1
Copyright — 2
Author's note — 7
Prologue, Part 1 — 8
Prologue, Part 2 — 14
1. Rose — 15
2. Moll — 18
3. Rose — 26
4. George and Alice — 28
5. Mother Abigail — 32
6. Rose — 35
7. George and Alice — 38
8. Kate — 42
9. Rose — 45
10. Doris — 48
11. Kate — 50
12. Stephen — 53
13. George — 56
14. Rose — 59
15. Moll and Phyllis — 61
16. George and Jane — 67

17. Rose	71
18. Alice, George and Stephen	74
19. Rose	86
20. Alice and Stephen	89
22. Stephen and Alice	98
23. Stephen	103
24	106
25. Bill and Stephen	126
26	131
27. George	139
28	143
Epilogue	148
About the author	151
Acknowledgements	152

AUTHOR'S NOTE

This book is about light and hope, even the black bits. Deep darkness makes us see how brightly the light shines.

Kevin Corby Bowyer
Thursday April 30, 2020, 5.33am

PROLOGUE, PART 1

Sunday December 1st, 1918

The scene: a military demobilisation camp in Flanders – noisy – bustling with British soldiers impatient to go home. George Cromack sits quietly, writing a letter.

My Darling Alice,
I can hardly believe it, but this horrible business is over and I can come home. I so very much want to see you again and hope that we can start afresh. My heart has been so full of sorrow these years that we have been separated. We parted very badly and I am deeply sorry for it. I wrote to you every week to start with, before I heard you had moved away. But now the war is over perhaps you are thinking of me as I am of you. I hope so. I have no address for you so I am sending this letter to my father in the hope that you may contact him. I have placed notices in various newspapers and periodicals asking you to seek him out. You know where he lives and this point of contact gives me hope that we shall meet again soon. Please forgive me my darling. I should have been a better husband and I deeply regret what happened between us.
I've written to Bill Hardaker and renewed the lease on the Boulby house from January. Every day I pray to our Lord Jesus that we will be reunited there.
I love you My Darling Alice,
Your George

Friday March 14th, 1919

At fifteen minutes past noon the passenger train from Whitby pulls into Boulby station on its way to Loftus. Only one passenger, Sergeant George Cromack, alights in the cold driving rain. The station is empty. There is no one to meet him. The emotional reunion he had dreamt about does not take place. As the train pulls out he adjusts his collar, fixes his hat firmly and takes up his bags. The street is empty – no sign of a cab or bus. His destination lies almost three miles to the north, mostly uphill. He begins to trudge his wet way through the puddles, out of the village and into the countryside, saturated fields to his left, the cliffs and the booming sea away to his right.

Just over an hour later the house comes into view. It appears dark and forlorn, a lifeless forgotten shell. Not for the first time George feels the sad weight of loneliness, the memories of happy times and the bitter regrets of dreadful mistakes. Boulby Cliff House is remote and isolated. Apart from their landlord Bill Hardaker, George and Alice had got to know only a few people – Doris Naseby (their nearest neighbour) and one or two of the farming families from whom they purchased food and milk.

George opens the gate and makes his way along the path, the vegetable beds to his right and the fruit trees to his left all overrun by weeds and brambles. He finds the door unlocked and lets himself into the hallway. Electricity has not yet found its way here and there is no gas supply in the building, but Bill has left an oil lamp on the kitchen table together with the house keys and a note welcoming George back. Striking a match, he lights the lamp and inspects the rooms. The house is dark, damp and cold.

The kitchen is small but houses a range, a sink with a single tap connected to the rainwater tank beyond the south wall of the house, a wooden table and two chairs, a dresser still containing Alice's crockery, a large bucket. A tin bath, usually kept in the outhouse, sits on the floor. He opens the door to the larder and finds a small quantity of food left for him by Bill, including milk, cheese, butter, a loaf of bread and a large pork pie.

The sitting room still contains the furniture that he and Alice had acquired around the time of their wedding in 1910. Two armchairs arranged either side of the fireplace, a small table, a wooden sideboard with shelf and mirror. There's no sign of his things – his books, professional papers.

George ascends the short flight of stairs and pushes open the door to the bedroom he had shared with Alice. Their bed is still there, bedclothes folded neatly at the foot. Once the heart of their life together it is now cold, loveless, vacant, dead. Total loneliness. George's face becomes wet with tears and he begins to sob deeply. As night closes in, the wind howls cruelly around the house and the heartless rain drives against the windows.

George's dreams are filled with Alice and his sleep is fitful and chill. The house, long empty, creaks around him in the dark. In the morning he lights the range with wood and makes himself a cup of tea.
During a brief pause in the otherwise relentless rain he dons his coat and hat, opens the back door and walks along the path. It slopes gently uphill, following the steady gradient of the land as it rises toward the cliff edge. The garden is very long and contains substantial plots of earth in which Alice used to grow flowers, vegetables, herbs and fruit. The potting shed is still there – Alice's home from home. She would sit inside during the warm weather and read, or drink tea. It is lit by windows on three sides and most of the garden can be surveyed from within. The greenhouse, its panes all filthy, sits opposite. The garden is overrun with growth now, uncared for and wild. George walks between the final two earth beds – the strawberry plot on his left, the bottom of the vegetable rows on his right – and stands before the low wall at the eastern end of the garden. Another hundred feet or so separates the garden from the cliff. Woods stand beyond the north and south walls, mostly oak and hazel descended from the prehistoric wildwood. The tree line is well back from the cliff edge, the trees themselves partly shielded from the North Sea gales by the incline of the land, although their manes have been sculpted and brushed back by the wind.
Gulls wheel on the updraft and the sea roars against the rock.

George wrote to Alice from the Front every week for several months but never received a reply. Bill, doing his best to look after his properties, began to intercept the mail to Boulby Cliff House in July 1916. He found all George's letters where they had dropped through the letterbox. The postmarks made clear their point of origin but Bill opened one and glanced at the signature just to make sure. He wrote back to George informing him that Alice had moved out of the house and away from the area some months earlier. Bill assured George that he would pass on the letters if, by any chance, she returned or made contact. He apologised that he hadn't written sooner about the vacant status of the house. Actually Bill was preoccupied with the fate of Henry, his own elder son, on the Western Front and had neglected much of his business.

He could not bring himself to tell George that Alice had moved away with Stephen Verrill, or that it had been Stephen, not Alice, who'd informed him that the occupancy of Boulby Cliff House was no longer required.

A few days after his return George asked Bill about the absence of his things. Even his clothes were gone. Bill explained that the house had been empty when he inspected it after the tenancy had been relinquished. That information made George very sad. Alice must have hated him so much that she felt compelled to eject all his belongings from the house, probably selling or destroying them. Well, he probably deserved it.

The months went by. April brought continuous and unexpected heavy snowfall. George took various labouring and farming jobs nearby, hoping for some news of Alice. Both her parents were dead. Her mother Esther had died giving birth to her in 1887. Her father Benjamin had died in 1911, a year or so after Alice's wedding to George. He hadn't remarried and Alice was his only child. There were no aunts or uncles. Consequently there were no surviving family members to whom George could turn for news of her.

One late afternoon in August, the summer sun blessing the earth at last with its warmth and goodness, he asked Bill to come and share some whisky. As the liquor began to take effect Bill's resolve to keep the truth from his host weakened. In the face of George's repeated requests for any clue that might reveal something of the whereabouts of Alice, Bill buckled and hung his head. He admitted that Stephen Verrill had written to him in February 1916 telling him that he would be leaving, taking Alice with him. They'd made plans to emigrate together to Canada, ending their tenancy. George was justifiably upset. His frail threads of hope disappeared in smoke. He stood up and asked Bill to leave, stating that he intended to move out the next day.

That night George wrote a note to Bill and left it on the kitchen table:

August 19th

Dear Bill,

Sorry about my behaviour this evening. It wasn't fair that you had to keep that information to yourself. I can see there was no easy way for you to tell me.
I'll have gone by the time you get this. If you do hear anything from Alice please let me know. I can be contacted via my father: David Cromack, Landcross, Bideford, Devon.
As for the contents of the house that belong to me. Honestly, I don't want to see them again. Sell them, or keep them for the new tenant – it's entirely up to you.
Thanks for all your help Bill. I hope you don't feel that I ill-treated you yesterday. Please forgive me.
All my best wishes,
George

Wednesday August 20th, 1919

It is a hot sunny day. George closes the garden gate behind him. As he does so he is aware of the fact that this is almost certainly the last time he'll see the house. He turns and scans it, the home that once resonated with so much warmth and affection. It glows in the summer heat but the building remains as empty of love as it was the day he arrived in March. She, who was once the most precious thing to him – she has gone – gone from his life for ever.
He turns, hoists his bag over his shoulder and, as far as he is able,

leaves his memories behind him.

PROLOGUE, PART 2

July 1755

The scene: the interior of a barn on Cappleman Farm, near Glaisdale, Yorkshire. It is a bright sunny day. The gloom in the building contrasts sharply with the brilliance of the sunlight beyond the wide open door.

Six year old Catherine squats in a corner. In her hands she holds a dead pigeon. Her fiery red hair falls forward as she concentrates hard and close on the bird's body. She sings quietly, stroking the creature – head, breast, wings, talons… It is not the first time she has done this – she knows how it works. She breathes her child's love at the creature, visualising it alive as she does so. The body warms in her hands, the eyes brighten, wings open – and the bird flies into the sunshine. Catherine laughs quietly in delight.

Her mother calls from somewhere nearby: "Kate! Where *are* you? Come *here* child, for pity's sake…"

1. ROSE

Monday November 22nd, 1965

Tommy Widdop drove his mail van carefully along the main road northwest from Whitby. It had snowed heavily and the roads were treacherous despite some attempt having been made to clear them. His deliveries had already taken him through Ellerby, Hinderwell and Roxby before backtracking to reach Runswick Bay, Staithes and Boulby. He would shortly deliver mail to the few cliff houses above Boulby village, then on to Easington. It was unusually cold for the time of year and he looked forward to reaching the end of his shift and putting his feet up at home in Carlin How. It was a long shift, though the villages were mostly quite small. Tommy had been delivering the mail here for nearly thirty years. He was one of the local "characters" and was well liked by all. Over the years he'd turned down several offers to move up in the postal service. He was an outdoorsman and liked his own company. He enjoyed his job.
Tommy slowed and took the minor road to the right, leading him toward the cliffs and the remote dwellings there. First on the list was Rose Headlam at Boulby Cliff House. Rose had been living here for longer than Tommy had managed the round. When he'd taken over the route in 1936 there had been three of them – Rose and both her parents. In 1945, when Tommy returned from active duty and was luckily able to get his old job back, there had still been three of them, but Rose's father, Edward, a trawlerman working out of Whitby, was killed in a disaster at sea in 1947 at the age of just fifty-four. The mother, Agnes, had died just last year aged seventy-three. Rose lived in the house alone, unmarried in middle age. They were a strange family, spoke almost never and were rarely seen. He wasn't aware of Rose's precise age. She looked older than her years, with fine silvery-white hair. If he'd not been aware of the ages of her parents at death, he would have estimated

her to be about Sixty. In fact, at fifty-one, she was just a year younger than him.

The minor roads were slippery and difficult but Tommy pulled in at the front gate, alighted and stepped carefully up the path. The door opened and Rose appeared.

"Tommy," she said.

"Miss 'Eadlam," he greeted her and handed over a small number of envelopes, all dull in appearance. No personal mail by the look of it. Tommy wasn't surprised.

"Thank you Tommy. Take care of yourself in this weather. It's not going to get better for a while according to the news."

"So I've 'eard. It's certainly worse than usual this year. These things are sent to try us."

"Sent to try us. Yes. Well, drive safely." She closed the door. Chattier than usual but still abrupt. In almost thirty years he'd never seen her smile: neither Rose nor her mother.

He went on his way.

Rose made her way back to the sitting room and set the mail on the table. The snow had begun to fall again and the room had become cavelike in the increasing gloom. Rose, sitting quietly as the dark deepened, found herself thinking again of her mother whom she missed very much, dead now for almost a year.

Agnes Headlam had been a kind soul. Agnes's own mother, Moll Forden, had been one of the family's great women, gathering much respect in her long lifetime. It was said that the eldest daughters had a special insight. Historically several of them had been respected as healers and there were many legends handed down through time both within the family and amongst those outside. For centuries they'd been tenant labourers on Cappleman Farm near the village of Glaisdale about thirteen miles from Boulby, but times had suddenly changed and Moll, her daughter Agnes, Agnes's husband Edward, and eight year old Rose had moved to Boulby Cliff House in 1923. The sudden move was engineered by Moll, the matriarch, who never discussed with them the arrangement she had made with Simon Flesher, owner of Cappleman Farm.

The Flesher family had worked the farm since the 17th century but the First World War had finished them off. Both of Simon's sons had been killed in the trenches in 1915 and '16 and his heartbroken wife, Maud, had descended into madness as a result. The big house on Cappleman Farm had been requisitioned and turned into a hospital in 1917 and agricultural activity had diminished. After the war Simon felt no interest in restarting work. He turned to drink, and in early 1923 had agreed to sell the house and a large part of the land. It was to become an asylum. The tenants had to move out – even those families who'd faithfully worked the land for hundreds of years.

The Boulby clifftop houses had to wait for electricity until 1952 although Rose still preferred to illuminate the rooms with oil lamps, finding it warmer, cosier. Despite her mild aversion to electric lights, however, she did enjoy watching television in the evenings. She also got into the occasional habit, late at night, of recording a kind of personal voice diary on reel-to-reel tape, and electric power proved essential for that too. On the evening of Monday November 22nd she sat in complete darkness as she always did, listened to the sounds of the house, and recorded her own voice:

"It's very cold, mum – and set to get colder. We had snow today and the weatherman says it'll get worse. The fridge is stocked, so I won't go hungry. I made some jam tarts this morning. Still not as nice as yours but I try me best… I don't fancy walking up to the bus stop – not sure if the buses are running anyway. Tommy did manage to get through with the mail today though – just the usual stuff. I walked down the garden this morning and looked out to sea. Very grey sky – couldn't see far. Few birds around, calling, wind, the sea crashing.
I do miss you, mum, I do – miss you – very much…"

2. MOLL

Thursday January 18th, 1923, 11am

The scene: Simon Flesher's office at Cappleman Farm, Glaisdale. Simon Flesher, aged 55 and owner of the farm, broken by the loss of his two sons, sits at his desk. Old Mary Forden (known to all as Moll) stands before him.

Simon: I'm not surprised to see you, Moll. I assure you I'm just as saddened at the way things have turned out as you are. You know, my family has lived here for centuries and my heart is heavy that our time has drawn to an end.
Moll: I feel for you Mr Flesher, I really do. But you must show more consideration for your tenants. It's not right to just order them to up sticks and leave, especially the families who've worked so long for you, and your father, and *his* father.
Simon: But – Moll, you must surely know – the sale of the land doesn't affect *everybody* living on the farm. The tenants outside the sale plot will stay here. They'll pay rent to me from the profits they make on their own produce – and they'll be working for themselves. If they can make a success of it things will work out well for them, and that is surely fair and reasonable. I like to think I'm a friend to the folks here, not just their landlord.
Moll: I know that sir – of course. But what about us? What about the Robinsons and the Flathers? Our three families will have to start again from scratch. I think you can do better for us. And I think you should. Our families have served this place loyally for decades – for generations.
Simon: Moll, I've done all I can. I've written favourably on your behalf to many of the farms in Yorkshire and I'm certain that something suitable will be forthcoming for all of you. You have three months to vacate your properties. I'm confident that something *will* turn up during that time (sigh). I know that you in par-

ticular Moll will be very much missed. I can do no more.
Moll: Mr Flesher (pause), in that case I'm afraid I must insist.

The comment stops him in his tracks. A kind of dark threat has manifested in the room. He is keenly aware of Moll's reputation and is fearful of what she might be capable. Flesher has heard the old stories and, like many a country man, is cautious about dismissing them. It would not be advisable for him, or his family, to be on the wrong side of such a person.

Simon (silent for a moment): Insist?
Moll: (no response, other than a small tilt of the head).
Simon: I know you're much sought after in these parts Mrs Forden. I would not wish to incur your ill will.
Moll: That is good of you sir. And wise.
Simon: What do you have in mind? Please be reasonable in your request Moll.
Moll: I imagine you're getting a good price for the farm – enough for you and poor Mrs Flesher to live out your lives quietly.
Simon: And the point...?
Moll: I think you should purchase modest properties for us, and also for the Robinsons and the Flathers – we three oldest families on the farm. It would be a considerate gesture in recognition of everything we've done here, and for your family, in all this time.
Simon: Moll, that would amount to a substantial sum.
Moll: You and Mrs Flesher will be free to live peacefully, without further toil. I think you should settle our families with similar consideration.
Simon: You mean money...
Moll: I'm not asking for great wealth – only a reasonable settlement as a parting gesture of goodwill – for these centuries of toil.
Simon (sighing): You ask a lot (pause). And, if I *were* to do this – what about me? Can you help me? My family? How much can *you* do for *us*?
Moll (shaking her head): Mr Flesher sir – Simon. Your boys are gone, and their bodies are far away. I can't do anything about that...

Simon: You can't? Are you sure? I've heard people say…
Moll: Trust me Mr Flesher. The stories about the things I do are exaggerated. You know how country folk talk. There's little I can do for you. And I know you're into the booze now too – that's a demon. I can't help you there – only *you* can overcome the drink. And your wife, Maud – I can't take away her despair. You'll both have to share the rest of your lives with that (pause). But I may be able to help with her ravings.
Simon: I would be grateful for that. Would you do that for me?
Moll: I will (pause). I'll come and sit with Mrs Flesher for an hour every day until the time comes for us to leave. I must have complete privacy for my visits. I cannot promise success but I will try very hard for her. Do you agree?
Simon: I do, Moll. And thank you for your kindness. It is appreciated.
Moll: And the other matter we spoke about?
Simon: I will make inquiries and set things in motion.

Moll walked back to the cottage she shared with her daughter Agnes, son-in-law Edward and their girl, little red-haired Rose. She trudged heavily, using her long wooden staff as support. A tall, weather-beaten woman, she was still strong at the age of seventy-five, though admittedly slower. Her husband James had been dead for twenty-three years.

There was a rumour amongst the country people for many miles around about a long-ago tragedy involving Moll's young sister, Phyllis. Dark stories were told, and the scent of necromancy hung close to all of them. The tales were speculative, and wild fantasies had grown up like the tendrils of a creeper, but no one knew for sure what had really happened. Except Moll and her parents. The three of them had to live with the memory of what had come to pass that day in August 1867 for the rest of their lives.

Maud Flesher had reacted to the tragic news of the death of her boys, Scott and Philip, with a swift descent into pandemonium. She screamed, threw things, smashed anything that was breakable, tore her clothes and injured herself – with a blade if she could get one. Her sanity swiftly withdrew, and only the regular application of barbiturates could restore any semblance of calmness. She was confined to her room. Her drug induced drowsiness produced rambling monologues directed at no one, and she had not resurfaced in almost seven years.

In the weeks following her interview with Simon, Moll Forden visited Maud every day. Their meetings were always behind closed doors and what happened remained entirely unknown beyond the fact that she insisted on the steady withdrawal of Maud's medication. Mrs Flesher never spoke of how things proceeded between them despite the oft-repeated curiosity of others – and no-one would dare question Moll. Maud's ravings did not return. Instead her sadness solidified into a stable dignity which, though sombre, allowed her to begin rational communication once again.

The improvement made in six weeks allowed Simon to hold his wife in his arms for their mutual consolation once more. His gratefulness to Moll showed in his tears.

Boulby Cliff House, 1923-1964

Simon Flesher was as good as his word and settled the three old families in purchased properties. For Moll, Agnes, Edward and Rose he bought Boulby Cliff House from its previous owner, Bill Hardaker, and made provision for the new occupants by way of a modest capital.

The building dated from the last years of the eighteenth century and had been vacant since early 1916, apart from a brief period immediately after the war when a previous tenant had occupied the house for a few months. The garden, untended for seven years, was wild and overgrown. The house itself needed some minor repairs, which Simon completed for Moll. He also extended the rear of the house and added a bathing room where a tin bath could be permanently housed without the need for hoisting it in from outside, as well as a convenient drain. A second outhouse was added against the rear wall of the house next to the coal bunker. On the upper floor of the extension he added a third bedroom, destined for Rose's occupation. The old outhouse was retained. Lighting was still by candle and oil lamp but the house was cosy and just big enough for its new occupants, who moved in on Wednesday May 16th, 1923.

They liked to keep themselves to themselves, although they were gracious enough to visitors. Doris Naseby called to welcome them soon after they moved in. Agnes invited her inside and they all sat down with tea and biscuits. Moll tolerated Doris for about five minutes before muttering an excuse and finding a seat by herself in the garden. Doris was still recovering from the death of her husband Harold two years previously and described their life together in the years they'd lived near Boulby Cliff. She was very taken with Rose, captivated by her bright red hair and hazel eyes, calling her "Rosie Red" over and over. Doris said they should visit High House, just over a mile along the lane, whenever they liked. They never took up the offer.

The family made contact with various local farms for the delivery of produce. Otherwise they led an isolated existence. Having previously been a farm labourer, Edward became a fisherman, working on a trawler which usually berthed in Whitby some fourteen miles distant. They never owned a car and travelling from the remote house was actioned by bicycle or, after the mile long walk to the main road, by bus. Thanks to Simon Flesher's generosity and to Edward's exertions at sea, they were quite well off.

Rose attended the small school in Boulby until she was fourteen. She made a few friends but rarely brought them home, and when her education ended in 1928 she lost contact with all of them. During her last two years at school she drew together a collection of twelve books that she liked to read over and over: *The Portrait of a Lady, Ivanhoe, Clarissa, Robinson Crusoe, Little Dorrit, Moby Dick, Don Quixote, Gulliver's Travels, Frankenstein, Dracula, The Mill on the Floss,* and *The Hunchback of Notre-Dame*. The volumes became Rose's friends. She set them on the bookshelf in her bedroom and imagined she could hear them breathing.

Rose liked to stand near the cliff edge beyond the bottom of the garden. She would close her eyes and enjoy the sensation of the wind on her face, the energetic fizz of crisp airborne sea salt, the song of the crashing waves, the shrill cries of the gulls.

Moll died in 1931 at the age of 83 and was the last of the family to be buried in the grounds of Glaisdale church. Her fame ensured a large gathering at the funeral, and her eight year absence from Cappleman Farm had encouraged the continued growth of myths and legends. A great healer, a woman to be respected and feared.

Agnes was liked well enough and was overwhelmed with the multitudinous good wishes of the people who came to see Moll off, but the country folk firmly believed that the powers handed down generation by generation had petered out and died with Moll. Moll was the last of them, they said. Her daughter Agnes had not inherited the gift, and having been married in a Christian ceremony she had evidently turned her back on the old ways. There would be no more such women.

The garden at Boulby Cliff House was huge and Agnes tended it largely by herself. Rose's interest in gardening came in phases. Sometimes she was enthusiastic, sometimes completely disinterested. Moll's gardening advice had extended only to occult pronouncements such as "Bury an owl's heart in the soil to keep pests out of the garden." Agnes would raise her eyes skyward and whisper, "and where am I going to get an owl's heart?"

When they arrived in 1923 the garden had been neglected for years and was completely out of control. Consequently they had to cut a lot of it back – sometimes drastically. Roses and various climbing plants strangled each other in the flower garden and the vegetable and fruit beds had gone wild. There was a bee hive by the south wall but it was empty, and the old chicken coop was rotten. Mould and filth covered the greenhouse glass and the trellises, poles and frames had mostly collapsed. It was clear that someone had once loved this garden with all their heart but it had gone to rack and ruin in neglect. In the fullness of time Agnes managed bits of it with commendable success and the three of them were able to enjoy its produce. The flower garden became Agnes's pride and joy. She cleaned and regenerated the greenhouse and potting shed, and the latter in particular became a favourite place for both Agnes and Rose. The hive eventually fell to pieces.

Seventeen-year-old Rose would often find herself at home alone with her mother while Edward was out with the boat. The war came. Edward Headlam, who was forty-six in 1939, was too old for conscription. In any case, being a fisherman, he had an occupation designated as a "vital industry". During the six years of the war many trawlers were called upon to help in the minesweeping effort, but about a quarter of all the boats were required to continue fishing, and Edward's was one of these.
Whitby itself suffered no air raids, although Rose and her parents, standing in the garden or on the cliffs behind the house, observed a few aerial dogfights between fighter planes. More than once German bombers returning home from raids on Hull dumped their unused bombs into the woods not far away.
Despite the unpredictable nature of conflict the family came through the war years intact. So it was still more of a shock when Edward was killed. The boat on which he worked struck one of the remaining sea mines. It was blown to bits and all lives were lost. Edward's body was one of three recovered and he was buried in Whitby cemetery in September 1947 at the age of just fifty-four.

As the years went by, Rose's brilliant red hair faded to copper and then to silver, although her hazel eyes remained sharp and bright. She listened to a lot of BBC radio and her accent picked up something of "announcer neutral", which became more deeply embedded as a result of her reading.
The passage of time brought mains water to the house and electricity finally arrived in Boulby Cliff Lane in 1952. Agnes took advantage of the technology to alter the house a little. She'd always wanted a bigger kitchen, so she divided Rose's old bedroom. Half of it became a new bathroom and toilet, complete with immer-

sion heater and hot running water. She had Simon Flesher's downstairs bathing room wall demolished and the kitchen extended into the newly opened space. The old range was replaced with an electric oven, and storage heaters were installed throughout the house. Rose moved into what had previously been the second bedroom.

They bought a television and set it up in Rose's small former bedroom. Agnes and her daughter sat together to watch the coronation in June, 1953. They never thought to install a telephone.

The television became the centre of their evenings together. On the evening of Saturday December 26th, 1964 sometime between 17.55 and 18.20, Agnes died in her armchair, quietly and unexpectedly. It was during the transmission of *Flashpoint*, the final episode of *Doctor Who: World's End*, in which the Daleks invaded Earth. With the Doctor's farewell to his granddaughter Susan still ringing in her ears ("During all the years, I've been taking care of you, you in return have been taking care of me…"), Rose looked across at her mother and realised she was dead.

3. ROSE

Tuesday November 23rd, 1965, 3.15pm

Rose sat on a wooden stool in the old potting shed, drinking tea and looking out at the elements. The sun had broken through the bleakness of the day, although the snow remained on the ground. She'd always been fond of the potting shed – there was something about it that warmed her, as if the devotion of earlier gardeners had been absorbed into its wood. Rose's mother Agnes had been such a gardener, tending the ground lovingly through the decades, growing food for them and filling the beds with colour. Agnes and Rose had often sat together here in the shed. Agnes used to think of the hut as the heart of the garden. It had been loved before and the simple honesty of that love remained here like the charge in a battery. It was an odd thing to say perhaps, but this instinct was not uncommon in the female line of the family. Moll would have sensed it too, and also the great women going back in the line – Moll's grandmother Abigail Storm, Kate Regan and perhaps others withdrawn still deeper into the past.

The sky gradually darkened. Rose took her mug, opened the door of the shed and made her way to the end of the garden. The distance from the house to the rear wall measured about 150 feet. The wall itself stood at waist height and contained an old iron gate that allowed access to the clifftop beyond. The gate itself was rusted and immovable, fixed partly open. Rose stepped out and moved as close to the edge of the cliff as she dared.

Although she'd lived in the house for more than forty years the impact of this view always took her breath away. She stood more than six hundred feet above the sea, the land sloping sharply downward and running into a sheer rock wall about a hundred feet below where she stood. Coastal erosion was an ever present concern. Altogether about fifty feet of the cliff top had been lost to the sea since Rose's family had moved into the house, thirty feet of that having disappeared in the early hours of February 1st, 1953, during the famous North Sea Flood. If the erosion averaged fifty feet in fifty years, the house itself would be in the sea by the mid twenty-second century.

The wind gathered force and the sky darkened further. There was a big gale coming in and Rose felt its threat. She turned and shut herself up in the house.

Rose presses Record on her tape machine. The recording captures the sound of howling wind:

"Hello mum. It's savage weather! I've never heard such a gale around the house. It's frightening. The house has stood for all these years but I wonder... I walked up to the cliff this afternoon and watched it coming in. The sea was really crashing and the water looked angry, with lots of white churning in the grey. The gulls were blowing about but the wind never seems to worry them much.

I wish you were here mum. It wouldn't be quite so scary if you were here.

No post today. I wasn't expecting anything anyway but I wonder if Tommy's still getting round the villages. The news says the weather's going to get even worse. Maybe they've stopped their rounds.

The house is very creaky. Sometimes sounds like there's someone...

Miss you, mum."

A few minutes before five o'clock Rose found herself awake. The building was trembling. The gale still howled furiously and her senses caught the end of a thunderous cacophony some distance away. Rose knew it could be only one thing.

4. GEORGE AND ALICE
Saturday July 23rd, 1910

The scene: The exterior of All Saints Church, Easington immediately following the marriage of George Cromack and Alice Eves. Arthur Filing, manager of *Filing's Photography of Whitby*, is taking pictures of the wedding party with his prized Kodak Brownie No. 2, Model B, while his boy, Peter carefully makes a record of the names of those shown in each photograph. George, dressed to the nines, looks the happiest man alive, his beautiful young wife Alice on his arm, a vision of loveliness all in white. George's parents, David and Sarah, join in the poses, together with Alice's father Benjamin, who has just given away his daughter to a young man he considers ideal for her. Sadly Alice's mother is not present, having died during the process of bringing her daughter into the world on October 29th, 1887. The summer sun, rarely seen that July, pushes aside the gloomy clouds and grants its blessings to the newlyweds.

Benjamin Eves ran a small bakery in the pretty Hertfordshire village of Standon, midway between London and Cambridge. His shop was just down the road and across the street from the mediaeval church of St. Mary, where he often read the lessons on Sunday. *Eves' Bakery* was a well-established concern and the delicious smell of freshly baked bread ensured a substantial queue most mornings.

His daughter Alice left school at the age of 13 to help in the business. She was a sunny, cheerful girl, always with a smile on her face and a gleam in her eye. She became popular at the counter and skilful at the oven. On Sundays she dressed smartly and accompanied Benjamin to church. Everybody loved her. The vicar wanted her to join the choir but Alice preferred to sit next to her father.

In his youth Benjamin had grown fond of the seaside resorts of North Yorkshire, particularly Scarborough and Whitby, and he often took Alice there in her childhood for summer holidays. He counted climbing among his other interests and frequently went on extended adventures in British mountain ranges. Snowdonia and the Grampians were his favourites.

In the summer of 1906 Benjamin met with a serious accident on Ben Nevis. He lost his footing on a steep slope and fell almost a hundred feet. Fortunately he was not climbing alone that day and his two companions managed to send for help. Benjamin's injuries had brought him close to death and he spent months in hospital before being sent home. Moving was difficult for him and he was no longer able to work in the bakery. Eighteen year old Alice looked after him during his convalescence but it was almost two years before he'd regained anything approaching his former state of health, and even then he was forced to walk slowly and with a stick. Alice had given him her whole life during the period of his recovery and Benjamin was immensely thankful for her. She filled the house with optimism and often sang as she went about her tasks.

Despite all the time she spent with her father Alice maintained a steady presence in the shop. She would often be found behind the counter, bright and happy, face speckled with flour. She kept the village smiling.

In the summer of 1908 Benjamin, feeling that he'd become a burden to her, began to insist that Alice should find a degree of independence. He suggested that she move, for a while at least, to the seaside towns where they'd often been so happy, and look for work there – and perhaps a husband and a life of her own. He offered to support her as she did so. Alice was both tearful and excited but agreed to go along with the idea.

Before long she'd found a job in a little shop in Whitby...

George Cromack was born at 11.21 on the morning of Sunday May 17th, 1885 in the Devonshire port town of Bideford where his father worked as a bank manager. He became interested in history before his teenage years and a keen fascination with archaeology followed. After school he found himself studying History at Cambridge – with considerable financial support from his father – and later joined a number of archaeological digs, including several in North Yorkshire.

Wednesday April 14th, 1909 found George in a Whitby draper's shop, having received a request from his landlady to pick up a parcel of cloth. Alice, aged twenty-one, was at work behind the counter. Their eyes met and she asked quietly how she might be of service. George had grown accustomed in Cambridge to the company of young women but this slender brown-haired blue-eyed girl took his breath completely away. He was so tongue-tied that he could not construct a simple sentence. She smiled and it made things still worse. Her eyes grew very large and she tried to stifle a giggle with her hand. George began to laugh too but soon regained sufficient control to deliver his landlady's message coherently, albeit smiling with delight as he did so. On leaving the shop, the goods under his arm, he was suddenly aware that he might not see her again, so he retraced his steps and boldly asked if they might share a table for tea at the completion of her days' work. She accepted his request and seemed pleased. They shyly bade each other *au revoir*. George's heart was pounding.

Within days they were madly in love.

Following the wedding, George and Alice Cromack had a small reception at nearby Liverton Farm. Their wedding cake had been presented as a gift by Harry Roth, Alice's employer, and the food was supplied by the kitchen staff of the Tiger Inn, Easington. A local group of musicians who specialised in such events provided the music and the wedded couple took their first dance together as man and wife. It was a happy day.

George had secured a lease on Boulby Cliff House and had moved out of his room in Whitby the week prior to the wedding in order to prepare the nest for his bride. At the conclusion of the reception the guests bade the couple "sweet dreams" as they were swept away to their new home by means of a chauffeur driven motor cab – a Belsize Roi des Belges Tourer, hired from Whitby. The evening was mercifully warm, and as the sound of the cab drew away into the distance George carried Alice over the threshold of the house to spend their first night together.

5. MOTHER ABIGAIL

Sunday August 22ⁿᵈ, 1841

The scene: Beggar's Bridge, Glaisdale.
Abigail Storm (grandmother to the as yet unborn Moll Forden) sits in a large wooden chair at the apex of the bridge. The chair is brought to this spot once each month from her cottage on Cappleman Farm so that "Mother" Abigail (now fifty-six years of age) can sit and receive her visitors. The acolytes who carry her chair stand guard at a distance as the afternoon wears on into evening. The river Esk flows calmly beneath the bridge and a light mist floats amongst the trees nearby.

Simon Overton, the parson of Glaisdale church, had an uneasy relationship with Abigail. He hesitated to use the term "witch" but the notion was always there in his mind. They spoke together civilly enough when they met but, to the clergyman, it felt like an armed truce. The country folk were in awe of Mother Abigail and her line and Simon knew there would be trouble if he were to go to war with her. His parishioners had many hushed tales to tell of both Abigail and Abigail's own mother, Catherine (Kate) Regan – and older legends were handed down in the local folklore. Abigail's daughter Margery did not seem to be one of the illustrious line. There was a belief that the "gift", as they called it, was handed down only through the females – and only if the firstborn was a girl. A firstborn son meant that the gift skipped a generation. Abigail's eldest was Eric, born in 1820. Margery, her second child, was born in 1827.
Simon had not been in post for long enough to conduct any ceremonies for the family and had been given to understand that the children were never presented for baptism. Apparently the "marriages" all took place amongst their own kind, away in a field or in one of their own dwellings. "Handfasting" they called it. They did

come to church for their funerals though, preferring the orderly burial of their dead, even in unhallowed ground, rather than disposing of the corpses themselves.

Abigail, on the bridge, receives her visitors one by one. At times there is a queue of people waiting. They bring their newborns to her for blessing, the seeds for their crops, their vegetables and other produce – even those items of furniture that can be carried here. Sometimes they come seeking a cure for illness. Abigail places her hands on them, whispers now and then phrases that sound like incantations, offers advice on what plants and growths to gather for healing purposes, how to prepare various substances, how to recognise the precise items required for the production of potions, salves, oils, liquids, pastes... She often allows visitors to her cottage and treats them in privacy.

Not infrequently she receives a direct request for something less tangible. In the old days some folk might have called these "spells", or "curses" – some folk still name them thus. Abigail always listens to such requests. She never smiles or mocks the applicant. Sometimes she issues them nothing but a fixed stare, sending them crawling away in fear. At other times she says that such things have passed away. But there are a few who are not disappointed...

"Mother Abigail..."

"Susan. I'm sorry to 'ear about your bairn." She puts her hand lightly on Susan's head, comforting.

(Sobbing), "He were jus' larkin' in 'trees like he allus does. 'E were reet up at 'top but 'branch brake and down 'e come – dead."

"I'm very sad for you Susan. I can't do nowt for you though. Dead is gone."

"But your mam, Mother Abi..."

"Dead is the end, Sue."

"Couldn't you just try, Mother? Your mother Kate, they say she..."

"She din't do nowt like that Susan. You go and forget that what people say."

"I'm beggin' you, Mother."

"I can't do nothin', Sue, 'cept help you and your man, Abel in your grief. There are some things that are so far away that, even if you thought you could reach out and grab 'em… it'd be against nature to do it. Evil things – you don't wanna go meddlin' wi' them. And I wouldn't wish your boy near 'em, dead or alive. Trust me. Things are better as they stand."

6. ROSE

Wednesday November 24th, 1965

The morning was clear and bright, the wind having completely calmed, though it was very cold. Rose opened the back door of the house and peered down the length of the garden. The snow remained, covering the earth beds and most of the path. The potting shed, greenhouse and the old outhouse stood unharmed, but the distant garden wall was not visible. Rose dressed herself warmly and pulled her Wellington boots on over her woollen stockings. Unsure as to how unsafe the garden might have become she set out gingerly, ready at any moment to turn and run back to the house – to the road if necessary.

The path seemed firm enough and her confidence grew a little as she walked along it, but the platform of land that should have been visible leading up to the cliff edge was not there, and the sea itself could be observed from the garden path. A substantial amount of the cliff had fallen away in the night, pulling the land immediately above it into a steady downward slope toward the precipice. The garden wall had entirely collapsed and the bottom end of the earth beds on either side of the path had spilled down the resulting incline. Beyond the garden, to the right and to the left, Rose could see trees leaning at precarious angles over the abyss, roots exposed like long fingers frantically searching for something to grasp, branches clawing the sky in precarious desperation, startled to find themselves confronted with the horror of a sheer drop where there had previously been solid ground. As she watched, one large tree in the outward curve of the cliff about four hundred yards away, gave up its hold and slid forward, roots pulling free of the earth. It tumbled over, plunging hundreds of feet down the rock face before hitting the new scree and rolling down the slope to join others that had already fallen. The crashing of the sea was very much closer, very much louder, as if proclaiming its triumph.

Rose was horrified. If the sea could eat so much of the cliff in a single night she would have to reconsider her estimate of the mid twenty-second century for the destruction of the house.

She looked around her, inspecting the wreckage. In the newly opened ground away to her left there appeared to be a number of objects of varying size and shape. Trudging carefully through the earth, and acutely aware of the dangerous new slope just a few yards to her right, she made her way to the spot and bent down to look more closely at them. They were bones. Rose knelt down, took a few into her hands and inspected them one by one. Some were long. She felt a thrill run through her as she realised these were not the bones of an animal. Somewhere there must be... She dug around with her hands. The soil was hard packed but had been broken up in the landslip so it was not long before she found, and dug out, a lower jaw. The remainder of the skull followed, teeth mostly intact, although there was a lot of damage on the left of the cranium – the eye socket had collapsed and several small splinters of bone were embedded in the earth nearby. In minutes a substantial amount of the skeleton lay about her. There were several unrecognisable scraps of cloth too, a few rags. Clothes possibly, or sacking? Rose's curiosity was fully engaged and she felt very excited by her discovery.

The necessity of summoning the police never occurred to her. Her family had been insular for generations despite the reverence in which Moll had been held by the country folk. Real social contact had always been very limited, and they harboured a centuries-old suspicion of authority. In spite of the fact that her nightly television diet had included *Fabian of the Yard*, *Dixon of Dock Green* and *Z Cars*, the reporting of her find was not Rose's first instinct. In any case she was completely isolated. There was no phone, she had no car, the bus stop was a mile away up on the main Whitby road and she didn't even know whether the bus would be running in this snowy weather.

Rose went to the potting shed and found a few tools to help dig out the remaining bones. She brought a bucket of warm water from the kitchen, together with a brush to help her clean the soil away, and then she worked vigorously, well into the afternoon. The disposition of the bones suggested that the body had been more or less intact before the landslip had scattered it, and it wasn't too difficult to determine the various parts – hands, feet, pelvis, limbs, etc. Rose was astonished at how many pieces there were – the spinal vertebrae and the ribs presented her with a few problems. Her instinct had completely taken over, and after several hours' work she was satisfied that she'd retrieved everything that could be found.

Rose knew, without making any conscious decision, that the body and the potting shed belonged together, so she carefully transferred it section by section to the wooden hut and arranged the pieces on the floor, the skull at the top and the other bones roughly where she thought they belonged. Whether the positioning was right or wrong the result did look like a human body, although one requiring assembly.

She closed the shed door behind her, sat down on her stool, focused her attention and began to sing, quietly and wordlessly...

Click...

"It's ever so late mum, but I wanted to tell you before I went to bed. Lots of surprises today. We had a terrible gale last night and a lot of the cliff come down. I felt the house shaking. The garden wall fell down and a couple of the beds opened up... There were bones mum, bones! Someone was buried at the bottom of our garden. All the time we've lived here – there was a man buried in the garden. I dug him up and cleaned all the bits. He's in the shed.

I look at him – I wonder if he can see me. I wonder how old he is – hundreds of years probably..."

7. GEORGE AND ALICE
1910-14

George and Alice lived happily at Boulby Cliff House. Harold and Doris Naseby, who lived in High House a little more than a mile up the lane, came to introduce themselves. They extended an open invitation to visit, but explained that they liked to travel and were away a lot. Albert Jackson, one of the local farmers, came by and offered to deliver produce regularly. Alice took a liking to Albert's young son Jimmy, who was always smiling and seemed to enjoy seeing her.

One Sunday each month they walked to Easington for the morning church service, a distance of about four and a half miles in each direction. It was a farming community and they stood out from the crowd a little but they were always welcomed. At home Alice was as cheerful and unselfconscious as she'd been when she worked in her father's bakery. George would often hear her singing or humming to herself, sometimes quietly, sometimes out loud. It rarely amounted to a real "performance" of anything although she had a lovely voice. There'd be snippets of the hymns she'd grown used to in Standon, or folksongs, or songs from the music hall. *The Bohemian Girl* was one of her favourites. The house resonated with her happiness. She made George smile.

George continued to work on archaeological digs in Whitby and elsewhere in the county, taking the bus to Boulby railway station and the train from there. His occupation meant that he was absent from home at times but Alice seemed content enough, especially with her beloved garden to nurture. They planned for a family but no children came, and a little seed of sadness began to grow in both of them. In his mind George could picture Alice as a mother. She would have been a wonderful mum, with a brood of happy little children.

Alice's father Benjamin died suddenly of a heart attack on Feb-

ruary 12th, 1911. She was heartbroken, having been so close to him. George and Alice travelled to the funeral in Standon later that month. Alice was too upset to stay in the house where she'd grown up so they took a room at The Star inn just opposite the church. So many of the village folk were pleased to see her, albeit under such sad circumstances. The church was filled. Benjamin had been a popular figure and his bakery had been part of village life for more than thirty years. He'd been only sixty-one, and his death left George as Alice's only next of kin.
They spent three weeks in Standon sorting out Benjamin's affairs and clearing the house. The process made Alice very upset but she selected items for removal to Boulby – kitchenware, bedclothes, a few pieces of furniture, books, several items that she thought probably belonged to her mother Esther, photographs. Arrangements were made for the bakery to be sold to the staff.
Before returning to Yorkshire George took Alice to Windermere for a holiday, where she began to recover a little. It was out of season and chilly but the complete break did them both good. They returned to Boulby in mid March and picked up the threads of their lives.

George, concerned that Alice might become increasingly despondent during his trips away, suggested that she might hire someone to help in the garden or with some of the household tasks. He would be happy to pay such a person. In his mind, George had formulated the notion that this individual would be a woman but his advertisement, placed in the local newspaper in April 1912, brought forth young Jeremy Silver, aged 14. Jeremy lived with his parents down along the coast at Staithes. He was a very enthusiastic and surprisingly knowledgeable young gardener and both Alice and George took a real shine to him. He was hired, and cycled to the house almost every day, a distance of some five miles in each direction. He loved his work and the journey kept him fit. Alice treated him rather like a son and George was delighted at how happy she was when they were gardening together. They became good friends. George and Alice called Jeremy "Jerry". Jeremy called Alice "Ally". Jeremy, always respectful, called George "Mr Cromack".

Jeremy worked wonders with the garden and got the best out of every inch of it, leaving Alice continually astonished. He treated the garden like the living, organic thing that it was, and he conjured with it like magic. Alice, who had previously done her best, really became his assistant. She watched and learned. The trees that ran from the front of the house and into the area along its north wall produced their finest fruit in response to his encouragement – apples, pears, plums, cherries, quince, walnuts and even peaches. The south garden, from the front wall to the back (a distance of some 250 feet) became a vegetable plot producing potatoes, carrots, turnips, beetroot, leeks, marrows, onions, cabbages and a variety of herbs. Jeremy's peas, supported on twigs, grew beyond the other vegetables, along with runner beans and broad beans on stout poles. The back garden on the north side became the site for the fruit – strawberries, raspberries, rhubarb, gooseberries, redcurrants and blackcurrants. In the area just beyond the outhouse Jeremy organised a second herb patch. The large plot in front of the north wall, behind the trees and beyond the fruit beds, became a flower garden – carnations, poppies, dahlias, narcissi, hollyhocks, delphiniums and peonies. Roses grew up the walls of the house itself. It was glorious. The long, upward slope of the land helped to shelter the garden from much of the wind and probably contributed to the success of the growth.

Before Jeremy's arrival Alice had tried to keep hens. It was lovely to have the fresh eggs every day but she became very upset one morning after discovering that a fox had got into their run and killed them all. She was distraught at the sight of their poor torn bodies and decided not to replace them. Jeremy understood her feelings and encouraged her to keep bees instead. So she acquired a hive and set it against the south wall of the back garden. A nucleus of bees was sourced and Jeremy gave Alice lessons in beekeeping. In time George and Alice were enjoying the best honey they'd ever tasted.

The three of them would often picnic on the cliff top beyond the garden wall. George would lie on his back under the summer sun, his face gently brushed by the sea breeze, a stalk of grass in his mouth, and reflect on how lucky he was. It was a very happy time. Despite his youth, Jeremy kept up an enthusiastic correspondence with many professional gardeners around Britain. In February 1913 he wrote to one of his contacts at Kew, expressing concern that the recent arson attack on the Tea House, carried out by suffragettes, might be repeated elsewhere in the gardens with possibly disastrous consequences for the collection. This led to an ongoing exchange of letters between several of the Kew gardeners and Jeremy that eventually resulted in an invitation to move south in order to join the staff at Kew. Jeremy was thrilled with the offer but very sad to be faced with the prospect of leaving Alice and the garden at Boulby Cliff. Of course, he had to accept, and on a sunny afternoon in July 1914 the three of them said their goodbyes. Alice shed a fair few tears but was very happy for him.

George placed another advertisement. Two weeks later they were interviewing Stephen Verrill, aged 18, who produced references attesting to his prowess as a gardener. Stephen lived in Loftus with his older brother, Robert. George did not instantly warm to Stephen as he had to Jeremy, but Alice, having become used to the company of a young man in the garden, looked kindly on him. Stephen was hired.

It was the biggest mistake Alice ever made.

8. KATE

Sunday May 16th, 1790, 9am

The scene: The darkened interior of a shepherd's hut on Glaisdale Moor. Candles flicker and substances smoulder in blackened dishes. Catherine Regan, mother of five year old Abigail, kneels beside a low bed on which lies the corpse of Amos Exley, dead suddenly at forty-two. Catherine mutters, hums little snippets of melody and works with her hands. Amos's body appears blue in the dim light.

His mother and two brothers wait patiently outside. A light wind blows across the moor carrying the sound of sheep from nearby fields. The dome of the sky is peppered with the subtly conflicting descants of birds.

After a while Kate appears in the doorway, a tall strikingly handsome woman in her early forties with flowing red hair. Her hands are aristocratic, the fingers long and elegant. She meets the gaze of the waiting family.

"What news Mrs Regan?" asks Miriam Exley.

"No news. Not yet. Whatever may happen next – the consequence is on you."

"Thank you Mrs Regan. I know you done your best for us. Blessings on you missus."

As Catherine strides past them in the direction of Cappleman Farm she points a finger behind her and says, "Don't go in there. Wait out here. If nothing happens by tomorrow morning sun-up burn the hut down and get on with your lives."

Miriam sits in the grass and watches the doorway. Her elder son John runs to fetch the other labourers from the farms nearby. Some of these hurry to the chapels at Glaisdale, Easington and Roxby, drawing people from the congregations as they disperse after the morning services. The respective parsons learn with horror about what the notorious Kate has attempted to do, but they know they must follow their flocks up onto the moor in order to see for themselves. If Amos rises their own credibility in these parts will be extinguished and the people will look to Kate as their only guide. On the other hand, if this hellish experiment fails they will be present to witness its failure, and will have the authority to denounce any fabrication that may otherwise take root.

During the remainder of the morning and throughout the afternoon almost two hundred people gather in front of the tiny hut. There is no movement at the door. They wait in silence as the sun goes down.

The night is clear and the sky is full of stars. The air becomes chill. A few fires are lit. Most of the children fall asleep in their mothers' arms. Sitting close together, the three clergymen begin to feel relieved.

The birds commence their singing long before the dawn. As the sun rises and daylight begins to fill the sky the watchers feel a communal sense of disappointment. The parsons smile and sigh. There is a gentle susurrus of activity as people begin to stand in preparation for returning home.

With a shocking suddenness all movement ceases and the field falls silent. The figure of Amos Exley appears in the doorframe.

Two of the clergymen hold their hands over their horrified faces, eyes blinking away tears of amazement. The third utters, "Oh, my God!"

Amos's mother walks towards the hut, her hands raised close to her face as if ready to protect it. Amos stands, unmoving. His eyes appear glazed and he does not acknowledge her presence. "Amos?" she says, but receives no response. He steps out into the low sunlight before she reaches him. His mouth is wide open and his two hands, claw-like, are held at chest level. He turns his head, and looking directly at his mother takes a loud and sustained indrawing of breath. He holds up his hands and looks at his palms. "No!" he says. Then louder, so that all hear him. "No!" He shambles forward. The crowd of horrified people part to let him through. No one follows. Even his brothers, appalled and fearful of the presence of evil, allow the husk of their brother to pass them by.

Soon Amos is over the brow of the hill, out of sight. All eyes concentrate on the point at which his figure disappeared, waiting for him to return or for some other event to take place. In the stunned silence nothing happens.

Adopting some authority, Giles Ottershaw, parson of Glaisdale, addresses the shocked onlookers. "Go home. What we have seen here this morning is the work of the devil. Pray to God for forgiveness. May all our sins be forgiven."

As the people depart the parsons face each other.

"That Succubus!"

"What's to be done?"

"We must together seek the support of Mr Flesher at Cappleman Farm. This witch must go."

Amos Exley was found the next day, face down in a pool of standing water on Roxby Moor, drowned.

9. ROSE

Thursday November 25th – Friday December 3rd, 1965

The snow began to fall in earnest during the night following Rose's discovery of the body. It was the start of several days of severe weather that would bring much of northern England to a standstill. Many roads became impassable. A passenger train became stranded in the snow in a remote spot some distance from Kirkby Lonsdale, having been forced to halt there earlier because of a blockage further up the line. During the later afternoon, as the depression moved away into the North Sea, northerly gales developed which, together with the continuing snow, brought blizzard conditions, particularly bad on high ground.
During all of this Rose sat in the potting shed talking to the bones, humming, comforting them with lullabies, recounting tales of her family including some myths from long ago. As the night came down and the real blizzard began she brought an oil lamp to the shed, relit her paraffin heater and continued her vigil, treating the body to lengthy passages from *Robinson Crusoe* and *Ivanhoe*. Rose trudged back to the house through the howling gale and driving snow almost three hours after midnight.

The following morning, the 26th, was bright and clear – a brief lull in the onslaught of bad weather, although it was still very cold. Rose dressed herself warmly in a thick coat, woolly hat and gloves, took a primus stove, paraffin, tea, milk, biscuits, jam tarts and more books into the potting shed, and nested herself there all day. The bright sunshine illuminated the interior and Rose continued to watch over the bones.
Her actions were entirely instinctive. She had no real idea as to their purpose. Her life in the house had mostly been an empty one, especially since her mother died. She had no need to work for a living, she had no interest in making the acquaintance of

her neighbours beyond the occasional polite greeting when the food was delivered or when Tommy brought the mail. Her family had never developed any real social skills and Rose wouldn't have known where to begin. So the body filled a space in her existence, brought her a companion. It had become a focus and she felt a fresh energy, an excitement that was totally new to her.

Heavy snow began to fall very early in the morning of Saturday, 27th and went on throughout the day. Rose, emerging from the back door of the house at 8am, found that she had to dig her way to the shed. Although the drifts were deep the snow was unusually watery. The door to the hut was barricaded by six feet of accumulated snow and drifts had piled up around the structure, restricting the ingress of daylight. The freshly lit lamp revealed the skeleton as it had been the day before, ready for Rose's attention.

Northern England had had little time to recover from the snowfall of the 25th, so the still heavier snow of the 27th caused utter chaos, blockading traffic and effectively keeping the country closed. The forecast predicted a big freeze overnight.

Rose had been looking forward to her beloved Doctor Who that evening. *Devil's Planet* was due to be broadcast at ten minutes to six that day, part three of the Doctor's latest battle against the Daleks. She apologised to the body in the shed, explained that she had a prior engagement, retreated to the house and made herself warm in front of the television set. The eerie music began and the titles came up, but the electricity suddenly went off and the TV picture collapsed to a tiny white dot. Unknown to Rose the snow that had gathered on the overhead power lines, now turning to ice as the freeze began, had become too great a weight for the cables to support and had brought them down.

She sat in the sudden darkness. "Bugger!" This voicing of an obscenity was rare for Rose, but she found herself unexpectedly disappointed and cross. She redressed herself for the outside, made her way to the shed, lit the lamp and shared her complaint with the silent bones.

Sunday the 28th was clear but very cold. The accumulated snow froze hard across the country. The 29th brought further heavy snow which settled on top of that still lying. Fierce gales blew up as the day wore on, driving the new snow into huge drifts of up to 14 feet. A wind speed of 50 knots (almost 60 mph) was recorded at Whitby. Two hundred drivers were trapped on the A1 in Northumberland. Miners were left stranded at Brandon Colliery near Durham because access roads were blocked. Some towns were completely cut off.

Up on Boulby Cliff the tempest was frightful. Rose, cowering in the shed, considered the very real possibility that the cliff might collapse taking the garden, the potting shed and herself with it, or that the gale might rip the frail building from the ground, hurling both it and her a mile or two out to sea.

Luckily no further damage occurred and the snowfall on November 30th was lighter. Wednesday December 1st was a clear bright day, though still cold. On Thursday there was a minor snowfall, although a thaw set in thereafter and the melt began on Friday, December 3rd.

Every day, and well into every night, Rose ministered to her silent friend in the potting shed. Nothing changed. The bones remained, still and dead, where Rose had placed them more than a week earlier.

10. DORIS

Monday September 7th, 1914

Harold and Doris Naseby were both in middle age and had lived at High House for some fifteen years. They were well off and liked to travel. Ocean cruises had been their greatest love but these had been curtailed with the arrival of war and their expeditions were, for the time being at least, confined to the home country. Their house was a rather more elaborate affair than George's, altogether bigger and with more impressive grounds. They were owners, not tenants.

On the morning of Monday September 7th, Harold opened his gate to assist Farmer Jackson in the delivery of foodstuffs to the house. Jackson's boy, Jimmy, following behind, carried a second box of produce. Father and son had just come up the lane after making a similar delivery to George and Alice.

Jackson greeted Harold. "Fine morning, Mr Naseby."

"Isn't it lovely? Do come in." Stepping aside to allow the two to pass.

"I see your old friend is workin' in 'garden at Boulby Cliff," said Jackson.

"Friend?" inquired Harold.

"Verrill. Stephen Verrill."

"You don't say. Really?"

"I do say. No good'll come o' that, I'm sure."

After the pair departed, Harold sought out his wife.

"Doris?"

"Yes dear?"

"You'll never guess who's gardening for the Cromacks."

"Tell me."

"Bloody Verrill."

"Stephen Verrill?"

He nodded. "Hm."

"My goodness! I wonder if we should say anything..."

Stephen Verrill had spent the summer of 1912 gardening for Doris. He had been just sixteen then. Doris had a suspicion that he was stealing small items from the house. She'd taken a dislike to him and had sensed untrustworthiness. One August Saturday, while Harold was away picking up a few things in Whitby, Doris told Stephen that she going for a walk with the dog. She locked up the house and set off. The dog appeared unwell and reluctant to go far so she turned and was back at the house in less than twenty minutes. She found Stephen "entertaining" a young girlfriend in the greenhouse. He must have had her hiding in the garden waiting for an opportunity. Doris was outraged.

"How dare you! What do you think..!" she began.

Stephen leapt up, and the girl quickly gathered her clothes and ran. Stephen muttered some curse and pushed past Doris, buttoning himself up as he disappeared round the corner of the house. He hadn't dared to return and she hadn't seen him since – good riddance.

"Maybe he's mended his ways?"

"Ye Gods, I hope so," she replied.

For several days Doris wondered if she ought to go down the road to Boulby Cliff and tell her story to the young couple. She really didn't want to bump into Stephen though, and the thought receded as the days went by. Perhaps he *had* mended his ways and grown up. Everybody deserved a second chance, didn't they?

11. KATE

Friday May 21st, 1790

The three local parsons, Harris, Ottershaw and Booth, are shown into the office of Henry Flesher, master of Cappleman Farm.

Flesher: Good day gentlemen. To what do I owe the honour of your visit, all three at the same time?

Ottershaw, parson of Glaisdale: You must have heard sir, of what took place on the moor this Monday morning past.

Flesher: I have heard a few wild stories. They are surely ridiculous.

Ottershaw: Not at all Mr Flesher. We all saw it with our own eyes. Amos Exley, who was dead, was raised through the evil intervention of Kate Regan. She is a witch and must be driven from these parts. In more enlightened times she would have been hung, or worse.

Flesher: That's nonsense, Ottershaw. There's been no execution for witchcraft in England for more than a hundred years. I'm disappointed that you bring such trivialities to my house. Why don't you confront Kate herself instead of running like bullied children to me?

Ottershaw: Because you, sir, are the master of this land. You have the right to revoke her tenancy. She lives on this farm with her husband Alexander, who is well aware of what she is and who does nothing to manage her. It is an outrage to us that she is permitted to remain – and an affront to God!

Flesher (rising from his chair): If you raise your voice in such a manner in my house sir, you will be ejected and not permitted to return! (pause). Kate!

Catherine Regan enters from an adjacent room, her fiery red hair flowing over her shoulders. Her beauty is intimidating. She is dressed in a claret coloured linen skirt and bodice trimmed with white. Her hazel eyes stare coolly at the clergymen as she walks slowly to Flesher's desk.

Flesher: Kate, what do you say to these accusations?
Kate: I wasn't even there.

The clergymen are silent.

Flesher (to the parsons): What is the current condition of Exley?
Harris (parson of Roxby): He's dead.
Flesher: So, he's dead.
Ottershaw (voice rising): But he was summoned back to life!
Flesher: Drivel. Who said he was dead in the first place?
Ottershaw: He was pronounced dead by the surgeon.
Flesher (raising his voice): Well, the surgeon was clearly wrong!

Kate appears to stifle a laugh.

Flesher: The people on the moor saw nothing unnatural. Exley was mistakenly pronounced dead. He later recovered, staggered about and eventually drowned himself on the moor. He was probably drunk. You know it wouldn't have been the first time.

Ottershaw is about to reply but stops himself. Perhaps this *is* exactly what they had seen. Perhaps the man was indeed only unconscious, not dead. Perhaps they had all made fools of themselves. It was possible. He looks at his two companions, both of whom are gesturing that, yes, Flesher's explanation might be correct.

Flesher: Kate, assure these men of your good intentions.
Kate: Masters, I am just a simple country woman. I mean no harm and no disrespect. I beg your forgiveness if I have offended thee.
Ottershaw: Mrs Regan. Do you give us your assurance that what occurred on the moor on Monday morn was no more than what Mr Flesher describes?
Kate: I do sir. You have my word. I swear it.
Flesher: Gentlemen. Explain to your congregations what they truly witnessed. There was no man raised from the dead. And there is no witchcraft – indeed, there never was.
Ottershaw: Very well, sir. We feel reassured by your words and

will withdraw. (To Kate) Good day Mrs Regan.

<u>Kate</u> (inclining her head slightly): God bless you sirs.

It sounds strange coming from her lips but her expression seems sincere. The parsons depart.

As the door closes Kate walks suggestively to Flesher, spearing him with her eyes. They stand face to face, and clasping her arms around his neck she reaches up and kisses him on the lips, at length. He crushes her in his arms, enslaved. She pulls back, smiling.

<u>Kate</u> (a little mockingly): Thanks, Harry.

<u>Flesher</u> (quietly, his eyes falling briefly to her cleavage): You vixen. You *are* a witch.

Kate throws back her head and laughs out loud.

Giles

Giles Ottershaw's nights had been filled with terror since that morning on the moor. He would toss and turn restlessly in his bed, sweating in fright, anticipating the clawing fingers of the shambling mindless dead in his flesh. He woke, as he always did, crying out and expecting to see a dark figure in the gloom of the room, hands outstretched, eyes sightless, crashing forward, lumbering foot by foot, lost, soulless...

The vision faded and he calmed himself as the stillness of the night returned.

Flesher's suggestion that Amos had merely been drunk was untrue – this was clear to Giles. He knew with all the certainty of his faith what Kate Regan was – and he understood fully what God required of him.

12. STEPHEN

August and September 1914

Stephen Verrill commenced his work in the garden at Boulby Cliff House on Monday August 17th, 1914. He was hired for fourteen days a month and tended the grounds with Alice as Jeremy Silver had. There was always something to do either in the flower garden at the side of the house, the herb beds or in the many vegetable plots. His references proved accurate and he applied himself with commitment and skill to the various tasks in hand.

In the early days of Stephen's employment, Alice found herself unexpectedly nervous of him. She became self-conscious when he was nearby and her spontaneous singing ceased. Stephen was after all older than Jeremy had been, stronger, more muscular. He carried a tobacco pouch and liked to smoke. In the hot weather he preferred to work without his shirt, and observing him thus from a distance Alice was a little fearful for her safety. She would be no match for him if he turned on her, and George was not always at home. But as the days wore on and she spoke with him at greater length Alice became reassured that his concentration was entirely on the garden. His imposing physical presence was simply the consequence of his being a strong young man. There was no reason why he should not be comfortable in his work, dressing himself in the manner he thought best suited to it. She forgot about it. In any case, she thought, why on earth would he have any designs on her? She was almost ten years his senior and probably appeared to him like a middle aged woman. In fact the reason that he felt so easy in partial undress before her was probably precisely *because* he felt no attraction. That reassured her. She felt rather silly and smiled at herself. She soon found herself humming quietly, then singing happily again.

Stephen was a selfish and manipulative individual and had been harbouring thoughts about Alice from the day of his interview. He sensed her early apprehension – knew that she feared him. But he was skilled in winning the confidence of others for his own interest and he plotted his course with Alice day by day. He felt her eyes on him in the garden and was aware of the steady easing of her misgivings towards him. But he would watch her also, admiring the grace of her movements, the delicate turn of her ankles, the softly pliant suggestions of her body through the fabric of her clothing as she knelt or walked, her long neck, the vulnerable innocence of her smile, her lips. She was like something made of the most delicate china. And he loved to smash things.

Stephen drank heavily with his friends in the public houses round about. He described Alice to them in lewd terms, telling them how he secretly spied on her as she undressed, and what he would do with her one day, before too long. The younger ones listened with their imaginations dripping. Stephen made the image of Alice into a kind of pornography for them and they looked forward to his stories with aching priapic excitement. Gilbert Rathmell and Albin Thackrey were Stephen's most dedicated listeners. Aged sixteen and seventeen respectively, neither of them had much experience with the opposite sex, so Stephen's tales of coital mechanics together with his vivid descriptions of female anatomy held a particular fascination for them.

The older members of Stephen's audience mostly despised him, with his repetitive stories of abuse and his self-aggrandisement. Bill Greenwood was one such. Bill planted himself on the outer rim of Stephen's circle and listened to him with disgust, considering his own principal function to be the protection of the younger ones. He was the antidote to Stephen, and at the age of twenty-nine, considerably older. His was the voice of dismissal, of common sense, although his rubbishing of Stephen's stories had brought about his own dubbing as a miserable bore – a jealous outsider who wished he had Stephen's luck with women but who remained terminally unattractive to them.

Bill had been raised in Kilmarnock by his mother, his father having fled in 1888 when Bill was just three years old. The neighbourhood in which he grew up was a tough one and Bill learned to defend himself well with his fists. Many of his peers allowed themselves to be led by the bottle but Bill managed to stay on top of it. He gained an early reputation as someone who was honest and dependable. His schooling ended, as was common, at the age of twelve and he went straight to work in the nearby coal mine. It was a hard existence but he keenly felt the need to support his mother.

Sorcha Greenwood was a strong willed and confident woman, proud of her son. She gained an income from a number of activities and was in part-time domestic service in one of the big Kilmarnock houses. Sorcha could support herself. She raised a sense of ambition in Bill and encouraged him to leave the mine behind, travel south and make his fortune, if he could. One May morning in 1905 he gathered together a few belongings in a bag, kissed his mother and set off on the long walk south to England.

Bill worked hard in the years that followed, although the hoped-for fortune never came. His first job out of Scotland was in a steel mill in Barrow-in-Furness. In some ways it reminded him of the mine and he found little satisfaction in it. He left after a year or so and became a farm worker in the Cumbrian hills. The outdoor work contented him well enough although he knew it wasn't likely to lead to the kind of success his mother wanted for him. He fell in love for the first time, but it was short-lived and his girl was coaxed away by one of the shepherds. Bill left.

He made his way to the North Yorkshire coast and took work as a porter at the railway station in Scarborough. Finding himself again disillusioned and unfulfilled he moved north to Whitby, where he supplemented his principal duties as a cemetery gravedigger with a furniture removal job. And this is where he first came across Stephen Verrill.

Bill was not a scholar, although he did read steadily and widely. He believed Stephen to be a psychopath, a danger to those around him. Bill disliked Stephen more than he had ever disliked anybody.

13. GEORGE

Tuesday October 20th – Wednesday December 16th, 1914

George's work in the final months of 1914 required a considerable amount of reading and research. He was well known in the Whitby Public Library and would often request books to be sent there from collections further afield. The rarer and more valuable items were usually restricted to the library premises themselves, and George consequently spent a lot of time in town.

During the previous year or so George's marital relations with Alice had cooled a little. The enthusiasm and vigour of their early relationship had declined as it became steadily more clear that a child was unlikely. They were still devoted to each other but the initial heat had subsided.

For his lunch George had taken to visiting a nearby tea shop – the Crocus Tea Room. He would give himself an hour over a light meal and a pot of tea to ponder his morning's study and smoke his pipe. As his visits went on he became aware that one of the waitresses had taken a shine to him. He would glance up and catch her looking quickly away as if to give the impression that he had not been the focus of her gaze. She would, whenever possible, make it her particular business to serve him at table. On one occasion he looked up from his meal to catch her, skirt lifted, adjusting her garter beside the counter, just within his field of vision. George was naïve enough to believe that the action had been unintentional. The girl caught his eyes on her and, blushing prettily, dropped her clothing back into place. She came straight over to him. George, feeling somewhat embarrassed and rather flustered, began fiddling with the newspaper he'd been scanning.

"I do *beg* your pardon sir," she said. "Please forgive me."

"There's nothing... I...." George was lost for words.

"Thank you sir," and she was gone, only to return five minutes later with his meal. "Bless you sir," she said.

George was back in the library that afternoon but found the intimate image difficult to get out of his head.

As time wore on the waitress's boldness increased. She would organise her movements and actions in ingenious ways that resulted in subtle display for George. She no longer allowed her glance to catch him, trusting that he was aware of her and that she was arousing his interest. George found that she was becoming the focus of his fantasies. On one visit in late November, as she was serving him, he asked her name.
"Jane, sir."
"Nice," he replied. "Nice name."
"Thank you sir." She lingered beside him for just a second or two. He noticed her scent and found himself a little intoxicated by it. He visualised her applying the perfume to her skin… without her dress…
He came to himself with a start. George realised that he was lusting for her. Yes – lusting, that was exactly the word. He was a little shocked and ashamed of himself. He rose instantly, and with a muttered apology to the girl, was gone. He found himself another tea room for his lunches.

On the morning of December 16th George kissed Alice goodbye and left Boulby Cliff House early. He was in Whitby by eight minutes to nine and making his way on foot from the railway station to the library. Unknown to him, as it was unknown to most people in the town, the Imperial German Navy had begun a raid on the Yorkshire coast an hour earlier. The fleet had divided into two, the southern half bombarding Scarborough shortly before eight o'clock while the northern half hit Hartlepool. The three ships assigned to the Scarborough attack then sailed north along the coast, finding themselves at Whitby by 9am. The battle-cruisers *Derfflinger* and *Von der Tann* opened fire on the coastguard station, with some rounds hitting the abbey ruins and the town itself. The shelling lasted for ten minutes.
The sound of the first explosions halted George in his tracks, and

others in the street looked around for a clue as to what was happening. Then something came rocketing through the air, whistling as it approached. The shell hit an end terrace house just along the street. As its roof exploded into bits and the windows blew out George noticed a cowering girl on the pavement opposite. She was thrown down by the force of the blast and George ran to her aid, brushing little bits of smoking debris from her hat and coat as they ran from the scene together. For the duration of the bombardment they crouched, sheltering in an alleyway, George holding her tightly to him for protection, his arms around her head and upper body.

After a minute or two of silence he relaxed. "I think it's over." He let her go and stood up, she following. He looked at her face for the first time. It was Jane. Something in him knew that it would be. She was silent but breathing quickly with the excitement of the moment. Her eyes were fixed on his. Her perfume mingled with sweat found his senses and he was overcome. He took her in his arms and kissed her.

14. ROSE

Saturday December 4th, 1965

The accumulated snow across northern England began to melt on Saturday December 4th, continuing for five days and causing widespread flooding.

Rose awoke to a bright morning and prepared a breakfast of tea and toast. The radio news informed her that ten RAF jet fighters had arrived in Lusaka in response to Zambia's appeal to Britain for help against Rhodesia. Harold Wilson had promised to send a battalion of six hundred Royal Scots Army infantrymen on condition that Zambian President, Kenneth Kaunda, agreed they would remain under British command, adding that action would only be taken against Rhodesia if hostilities escalated. The Beatles album, *Rubber Soul* had been released the day before. The spacecraft Gemini 7 was scheduled for launch into orbit from Cape Canaveral later in the day. Ike Richman, lawyer and co-owner of the Philadelphia 76ers basketball team, had died while sitting on the bench during a game against the Celtics. The weatherman told her that no further snow was forecast.

Dressing up against the cold and donning her boots in the usual manner, Rose made her way, munching on toast and jam, to the potting shed. She shut the door behind her and lit the lamp to illuminate the floor more clearly.

There was something different about the collection of bones. Rose peered and couldn't immediately see what it was. Then she realised they appeared darker than before. The grey and dull brown of the earth in which they'd been buried had become a more uniform colour, almost black, and they appeared to be slick with liquid. Rose reached down and took up what she believed to be one of the shin bones. It was indeed damp. Her fingers came away wet and she rubbed them together, feeling the moisture. She sniffed her fingers, then the bone, but was unable to detect any scent other than the earth from which the bones had originated. "Water," she said to herself. The rational part of Rose's mind told her that the melting snow must be seeping into the shed and the dry bones somehow sponging it up. She didn't know much about how such things might work, though she was prepared to accept that logical explanation.

Another part of her jumped to a different conclusion though, and she again concentrated hard and began humming to the bones.

The shed was like a cocoon. Outside the melt continued, the garden filling with the gentle sounds of the dripping, trickling, plopping of the thaw.

15. MOLL AND PHYLLIS

Abigail Storm gave birth twice. Both were Wednesday children. First Eric, on March 1st, 1820, then Margery, on January 10th, 1827. Margery, being the second born, did not inherit the powers vested in Abigail. Indeed, her mother was happy that it was so – Margery would be able to live a normal life, without Abigail's special responsibilities.

Margery wed Jacob Foster (her senior by one year) on Friday August 20th, 1847 at the tender age of twenty, already with child. Mother Abigail died in 1866 at the great age of eighty-one, living long enough to welcome into the world both of Margery's children. Mary (who was called Moll from her earliest days) was born on Thursday January 27th, 1848. Phyllis, a great surprise to everyone and a delight to Margery, was an unexpected late addition to the family, arriving on Friday July 19th, 1861, a full thirteen years after her sister.

Phyllis was the apple of her mother's eye, such a delayed and unexpected gift receiving the full attention and love of a mature parent. In light of this, the terrible events of late August 1867 were rendered still more tragic.

Sunday August 25th – Wednesday August 28th, 1867

It was a children's game gone wrong. Nineteen year old Moll had been given the task of looking after six year old Phyllis for the afternoon. Jacob, father to the girls, was working in the fields and Margery had an afternoon of visits and tasks to perform around the farm. Moll took her sister and her sewing to the well and settled herself on the low wall, next to the crank handle. Phyllis played happily with her doll. It was a warm day and Moll felt the refreshing cool of the well shaft at her back. She leaned over and called into the gloom, enjoying the echo that returned.

Phyllis laughed at the sound and came to join her sister. She looked over into the dark depths and cowered back in fright at the drop she saw. The well was not deep – less than twenty feet – but to the little girl it looked scary enough. Moll smiled and shouted into the well. The echo came booming back and she laughed. Phyllis, infected by Moll's hilarity, held her doll over the well shaft, leaned forward and called into the void, enjoying the returning sound of her own voice. She began making small, thrusting runs at the well, shouting louder at each approach and holding the doll before her at arm's length, leaning over further each time. Suddenly Moll became aware of the danger, and crying out "That's enough, Phyl," dropped her sewing and put out her hands to quell her sister's excitement. But it was too late. Phyllis overbalanced on the wall and disappeared over the edge. She squealed as she fell, and a second later came the sound of her little body hitting the water.

There was silence. Moll was horrified, and her hands flew to her face. Peering into the darkness of the well she could faintly see her sister lying at the bottom. Phyllis appeared to be lying face down in the water and exhibited no movement. Moll, in a panic, shouted down the shaft. The sound brought others running. Several people had been working within earshot but none had seen what had come to pass. Despite their many calls and shouts Phyllis's body remained immobile.

Someone suggested that a man should climb down on the bucket rope but another pointed out that the mechanism, or the rope itself, would probably not hold the weight of a person. They sent a runner to find a good strong cable or a long ladder, and minutes later he returned with a thick reel of sturdy rope. A number of the onlookers held it firm while Alfred Meale, one of the farm labourers, descended into the darkness. He lifted Phyllis from the water but could detect no sign of life. Calling up, he instructed those above to find a sack. Some time later Phyllis's body was recovered. She was dead, her head angled strangely, neck broken.

Moll, feeling fully responsible, was distraught, and Margery, having been called from her rounds, was inconsolable with grief. Phyllis's sodden, shattered body was carried to the family's cottage and laid on her bed. A surgeon was summoned and the child was formally pronounced deceased. Her mother and father wept on their knees beside her corpse. Moll felt lost and soulless.

Within hours a small wooden coffin arrived and was mounted on trestles in the parlour. The undertaker placed Phyllis's body inside it and the parson was summoned so that funeral arrangements could be made. Margery and James kept vigil at the coffin all night. Moll, heartbroken and shut in her room, did not try to sleep.

In the black of the night she began to ponder. She had some awareness of her family's past. Her grandmother Abigail had been considered the wise woman for miles around, holding court for decades from her chair on Beggar's Bridge and up on the moor. Folk would often come to the house seeking substances, oils and the like or to have their cards read. There were many stories of how she would heal animals with her hands, though no one could explain exactly how this was achieved. The local people liked Abigail's daughter, Margery, although they knew she was not a healer like her mother.

But the stories told of Kate Regan, Moll's great grandmother, had gained heroic status. When the country folk round about used the word "witch" it was Kate they meant. The term was used in awe, and the dark tales spun about her were recounted in hushed tones amplified by gestures of wonder and amazement. A great beauty they said, a terror, who once resurrected a man from the dead.

The circumstances of Kate's own death were shrouded in mystery. In 1797 she'd been found on the moor near the village of Beck Hole, unclothed (so the story went) and shot to death, having sustained wounds at close range from twenty-one musket balls. Forty-eight years old she was survived by her husband Alexander, who brought up twelve year old Abigail alone. In the seventy years since her death Kate Regan had acquired the triple status of the county's greatest beauty, heroine and demon.

Moll knew in her heart that she herself was one of her line's special women. Some of her earliest memories involved watching Abigail at work, recalling the actions of her hands, listening to her murmurings. Her grandmother had passed on some knowledge to her but Moll's own self-awareness enclosed a deeper, instinctive sense of the power she had inherited. It resonated with the secrets of the natural world and energised her. Catherine Regan, some said, had the power to reverse death. Having already lost so much, Moll focused her attention on that legend.

The funeral was planned for noon on Wednesday August 28th. On the preceding night, Jacob managed to convince Margery that they should try to sleep. Moll reassured her mother that she herself would keep vigil over Phyllis for the night.

Moll had planned her occult procedure as best she could, never having learned how such a thing might progress but trusting largely to her inner knowledge. The worst outcome would be if her parents discovered her during the process. They would probably be horrified and she would get a scolding, followed by forgiveness as they acknowledged to what acts of desperation Moll's own despair had driven her. At best – they would get Phyllis back, alive.

The night set in, the fire flickered, and Moll attended to her dead sister. She was busy for hours, and the dawn light, peeping over the rim of the moor, found her collapsed in exhausted sleep next to the coffin. Phyllis lay as dead as the night before.

Margery came into the room an hour or so later, and seeing Moll motionless on the floor feared she'd lost both her children. Her cry summoned Jacob and the two of them quickly brought Moll to consciousness. Water was fetched and she was soon fully revived. Finding her feet and looking into the coffin Moll discovered that her efforts had achieved nothing.

The three of them sat together for a sombre breakfast of bread, butter, cheese and jam, although very little was consumed. Margery made tea, most of which cooled and was thrown away. Few words were spoken, the atmosphere in the house being overwhelmed by the presence of death.

They dressed for the funeral and made themselves ready for the arrival of the cart upon which the coffin would make its journey to Glaisdale church, where old Simon Overton would conduct the ceremony prior to burial in the churchyard. In the few minutes remaining the three of them stood around Phyllis to make their final farewells, the coffin lid propped on end by the fireplace, ready to be lifted into position and screwed down.

Phyllis opened her eyes. Glancing around she quickly found her mother and tried to lift herself up, but her arms were broken. Margery, shocked almost to death, cupped her face in her hands and Jacob muttered, "My God..." Phyllis began to gurgle and a small quantity of sticky blood-laden fluid spilled from her lips. After a few seconds her eyes glazed in a second death and she collapsed where she had lain.

The sight was pathetic beyond words and Moll was appalled – this was not one of the outcomes she'd anticipated. "Phyllis...?" She remained standing by the coffin, failed in her task. Her parents gathered some semblance of their wits together and Margery addressed her daughter.

"Moll?"

"I'm sorry. I wanted her back." It was only then that she began to vent her sorrow in tears. Margery comforted her and Jacob also gathered himself together. The knowledge of past events in their family history provided some protection against the horror of the occurrence and, being her mother, Margery had been well aware that the gift had lodged itself in Moll. Appalling though it was, the event was not entirely without precedent.

The cart and mourners arrived, the funeral went ahead, and Phyllis was laid to rest in the earth with her ancestors. Neither Moll nor Margery ever spoke of what had occurred.

The loss of a child is an event that tears a permanent hole in the lives of the parents left behind but Margery was able, in the years that followed, to channel her grief into something worthwhile. She concentrated all her efforts into nursing and became a companion to the elderly and infirm. The affection in which she was already held in the local communities flourished into a real love as time went by. "Send for Margery...", "Margery will know what's to be done…" – such utterances became commonplace. She died in 1899. Her funeral packed Glaisdale church. Three hundred additional mourners waited outside. It was the biggest committal the parish had ever seen.

But Jacob was increasingly unable to bear the memory of what had occurred. He became morose and a deep depression set in. One morning in January 1868 he walked out of the cottage and never returned.

In July 1869, at the age of twenty-one, Moll married James Forden. In the ensuing years she became the wise woman of the country folk and enjoyed a long life, respected and revered by all. Jacob, having removed himself from Margery, Moll and the farm, fell into lonely insanity and mumbled about broken children, sightless corpses and the devilish resurrection of the dead, adding to the stock of folklore handed down concerning the line of Kate Regan.

16. GEORGE AND JANE

Wednesday December 16th, 1914 – Tuesday January 12th, 1915

George, horrified at himself for the spontaneous passion of that first kiss with Jane, tried to pull away. He attempted weakly to apologise but she was already kissing him again. The excitement and danger of the bombardment had heightened their senses and George found himself almost beyond control, opening her coat and hungrily hoisting her skirt. The only thing that prevented them going any further was the fact that they were in an alley, with people running by just a few feet away, seeking cover in case the shelling continued. George, with a considerable effort, pulled himself together. Jane was still grasping him tightly, arms around his neck and trying to kiss him, but George managed to dislodge her.
"My God, I'm sorry. Look, I'm married. I mustn't…"
She withdrew, breathless, lips parted, and began to rearrange her clothing.
"It's not your fault. I wasn't thinking," she said.
They both began to calm down.
"Are you all right?" he asked.
"Yes, yes. Are you?"
"Yes. Let's find somewhere safer."
A pause, then: "You haven't been to the Crocus recently."
"I know, I…"
"It's me, isn't it?"
"No… Yes. Look…"
"Come now and sit quietly for a while. It'll be as safe as anywhere. I'm on duty soon – if the shop is to open. It'll calm you down."
"All right."
A few minutes later they were facing each other across a table prior to the start of her shift. Now that things were calmer he felt much easier in her company, having been able to pull back from

the vertiginous sexual precipice over which he had so nearly fallen. She seemed happy, smiling. George thought she was rather lovely.

Normal life began to resume as they sat there. People walked about as they usually did and the limited damage was cordoned off for safety. George went to his work in the library but Jane was on his mind all day. The sensation of her body in his arms was a memory very difficult to dislodge. That night, at home in Boulby Cliff House, Alice was surprised by the energy George brought to bed. She thought it must have had something to do with the emotional aftermath of the naval attack. Of course, George was thinking of Jane...

Lunchtime the next day found George again in the Crocus. Jane was very happy to see him and they started to feel like old friends. The meetings were repeated in the days that followed.

On the Tuesday after the attack, when she was off duty, they took a train to Scarborough and spent the day together, wrapped up against the cold. She asked about Alice and he told her their history. Jane Grainger had no romantic companion and lived alone with her mother. She led a simple life: church on Sundays, work during the week. At twenty-two years old, she was eight years younger than George. Jane asked him point blank if he loved his wife. George told her yes – he did. Jane and George felt very close to each other but locked beyond reach by circumstances. They held hands on the way back to Scarborough railway station and sat very close to each other on the journey to Whitby. George thought how easy it would be to find a room somewhere, turn down the lights and forget the outer world. Before they parted he kissed her on the cheek. She returned the kiss on his lips, held his face in her right hand and smiled deeply into his eyes.

"George," she murmured.

He felt the last of his defences falling. "I must go. Have a lovely Christmas, Jane." With a tremendous effort he turned and made his way to the Boulby train under the blind gaze of a multitude of finger-pointing Lord Kitcheners.

George and Alice spent Christmas and the New Year in Bideford with George's parents. They were happy together and George felt his emotions recovering from the time spent with Jane. David and Sarah Cromack had always liked Alice and thought George had been very lucky to find such a suitable match. She was a delicate, graceful girl.

It was the last festive season that George would spend with Alice and also the last he would spend in the company of his mother.

They returned home on Monday January 4th, opening up the cold house after their absence of almost two weeks. The grounds were mostly dark although the happy little snowdrops were out, lending a myriad spots of white eagerness to the wintry earth. Within the soil the garden was already preparing for the new year. George was thinking, with some excitement, about returning to work the next day.

He'd gained a reputation as a researcher and field worker and conducted many of his activities on a freelance basis. He would find himself contracted to various local authorities, historical organisations, museums, research institutions, archaeological societies, field units and trusts. He travelled a lot, and had one more week to spend in Whitby before moving on to an excavation in York.

The following lunchtime found him back in the Crocus. He and Jane agreed to meet for a drink in the early evening after her shift was over. Half past five found them in the Britannia Inn on Church Street, a popular pub on the bustling east side of the harbour, close to the water. They were very warm toward each other. An onlooker would have thought them young lovers, and in many ways that is how they began to think of themselves.

It was a stroke of bad luck that Stephen Verrill was drinking in the same pub that evening. He watched them from a distance. Their smiles, their eyes, the soft touching of each other's faces, all indicators of a relationship of physical intimacy. When they parted company an hour later it was with a kiss. They held each other briefly and their lips met. Stephen stored all this up for later use.

George felt anxious and guilty about his secret, aware that he was being dreadfully unfair to Alice. But he knew that he was enslaved by his infatuation. Feeling powerless to deflect it he made up his mind, in spite of all his misgivings, to allow it to run its course. He asked Jane to take a couple of days off and come with him to York. Understanding immediately what that meant she promised to make the arrangements.

They met regularly in the Britannia in the days prior to their departure for York on Monday 11th. George had bought railway tickets and booked their hotel room. It seemed there was no going back and the anticipation kindled a frisson, a thrill, between them that might have been palpable to an observer.

And indeed it was so. Stephen hid away from them in the opposite end of the pub, keeping the crowd of drinkers between the couple and himself – watching as their relationship approached boiling point.

The next Monday George kissed Alice goodbye and travelled to Whitby railway station where he met Jane. During the journey to York it was as much as they could manage to control themselves and sit calmly together side by side, her hand in his, their bodies pressed as closely as possible in the carriage. George's heart was beating so hard with excitement and anticipation he thought he might die.

That night and the next, Stephen Verrill, hoping to continue his spying, waited in vain.

17. ROSE

Sunday December 5th – Wednesday December 8th, 1965

The thaw continued and the drifts of snow in the garden at Boulby Cliff became less and less. The ground was sodden with slush and run-off.

There was a gradual evolution on the floor of the potting shed. Exactly what was going on Rose did not know. Perhaps it was the result of many things – the stored energy in the structure itself that she, her mother and old Moll had all been aware of. Maybe Rose's own daily devotions had something to do with it. Or perhaps there were deeper, unfathomable, forces at work, in the earth, in the heavens – who knew? Probably a combination of all these things and more.

On Sunday Rose arrived in the shed to find that a black substance had begun to grow on the surfaces of many of the bone pieces. At first she thought it was mould, encouraged by the new dampness of the earth. As the day went on an odour began to arise from the skeleton, faint at first but stronger as evening approached. It was a curious scent, not unpleasant, a little like spring growth.

The action seemed to accelerate after that. On Monday morning Rose found that the substance had begun to connect one bone to the next, drawing the separate pieces subtly together. Rose sat in the potting shed all day trying to catch signs of the ongoing development. From time to time she was aware of gentle scraping sounds on the wooden floor. By evening the pieces had all joined and the appearance of the bones had begun to resemble a dead body rather than a mere skeleton.

At 2.15am, when Rose tore herself away in order to sleep, she spoke to the body: "I'll see you in the morning my love. Wait till I come. Don't leave without saying goodbye."

On the morning of Tuesday 7th Rose found that the tissue on the body had thickened. All the pieces had firmly gathered themselves together. She knelt down and examined the corpse. The flesh (if that was what it was) was cold and hard, as if mummified. Investigating the head, she found that the collapsed left side had developed a firm layer of what appeared to be skin, partly covering the cranial damage. Rose ran her hands over the body lovingly. "You come to me my dear. Come to Rose. I'll take care of you. Come home my love."

As the day wore on the tissue thickened and most of the remaining cavities filled. Again Rose went to bed very late – after a brief taped message to her mother recounting the developments.

On Wednesday December 8th Rose overslept. She'd left her bedroom door open as she often did and was awakened at quarter past ten by the sunlight streaming through the bathroom window across the landing. Rose was instantly concerned that her friend in the potting shed might think she'd lost interest. She pulled on her boots and made her way to the hut without stopping for a cup of tea. The body was still there on the floor, all black, rather shrivelled, though fully intact. For the first time Rose could see it was a woman.

The head appeared to be complete, the left side seemingly reconstructed and exhibiting only minor traces of the damage that had previously been plain. The body was still dry and hard when Rose arrived that day but gradually softened as the hours wore on. Its skull had developed ears and eyelids, though the cartilage of the nose failed to appear, leaving a triangular hole in the middle of the face. Lips were present, fused together in a sad line. Later, the body's fingers and toes began to show signs of nails.

In the afternoon small thin patches of hair began to appear on the head. Rose caressed the body all day, singing to it and assuring it of her love. She read a few passages from *Moby Dick*. Its tissues softened gradually and began to assume the texture of someone more recently dead, while its skin colour lightened a little to something approaching that of drying peat.

In the afternoon the weather turned, becoming overcast. A thin rain fell for several hours, washing away the last of the snow, but at nine thirty in the evening the clouds parted and the glorious silver disc of the full moon came shining through. Silvery light flooded the interior of the potting shed, overcoming the dim illumination of Rose's oil lamp. With the kiss of the moon Rose sensed a second presence in the shed. Peering down at the body she saw that the dark dry eyelids were slightly lifted. The woman on the floor was looking at her.

18. ALICE, GEORGE AND STEPHEN
Wednesday January 13th – Friday July 23rd, 1915

George returned home on the evening of Wednesday January 13th. Alice greeted him with a kiss and asked how his visit to York had gone. George described his work at length but withheld the peripheral details of his time away.
"Did you enjoy the city?" asked Alice.
"Yes, it's a lovely place. You get a real impression of the mediaeval town – and the Minster is glorious of course."
"If you're going again perhaps I could come too?" Alice did accompany George from time to time so the suggestion brought no surprise.
"Yes," said George warmly. "That would be nice."

On the second of his two days away with Jane, George had become overwhelmed with remorse. It was the first time he'd been unfaithful to Alice. Jane instinctively knew what was wrong and did her best to comfort him.
"I understand, George," she said. "You and me – it will only work if you're happy."
"You're such a sweet girl Jane. I've abused you horribly." He was shedding tears because of her kindness to him.
"Try not to judge yourself harshly love. Be calm. You'll do what's right, I know you will."
Silence for a moment. Then, "Do you love me, Jane?"
She hesitated for a moment. "Now's not the time to ask me that, George. It'll only make things more difficult."
"Yes, of course." Taking her hand: "You're so kind Jane. I treasure you."
But on the journey home George more or less made up his mind that his brief affair with Jane must come to an immediate end. Before they parted at Whitby railway station he held her in his arms.

He was acutely aware of the warm softness of her body, his own having been so recently enfolded in its secrecy. His intoxication with her made it very difficult to pull away. George told her to expect news from him soon.

Alice's suggestion that they should visit York together had contributed to his final decision to end things with Jane. It conjured in George a firm awareness of himself and Alice as one, reinforcing his sense of union with her alone.
The next day George told Alice that he'd forgotten some essential work and that he would have to spend the afternoon in Whitby. Leaving on the noon train from Boulby he was in the Crocus tea room by twelve forty-five. Jane was very pleased to see him and George thought his heart might break. She felt the restraint in his greeting but, sensing what was to come, agreed to meet him in the Britannia at half past five.
They sat together at their usual table and talked for half an hour. Jane wept a little, and holding her hands across the table George felt dreadful. She did not plead with him, did not beg him to reconsider. Her dignity made him feel even more wretched. They parted at six o'clock, holding each other tightly in the street before going their separate ways, both in tears.
Stephen hid and watched.

In the ensuing weeks George tried, with limited success, to rid his mind of Jane. He wore a contented face at home but Alice knew that something was wrong. There had been a further, sudden deterioration in their physical relationship – a clear withdrawal of interest. He never sought to love her during the day and his nocturnal embraces had become cool and routine. Now and then she asked him what was wrong but he always replied that it was nothing – he was just tired. Alice grew steadily more concerned.
At the end of February George's mother Sarah died suddenly in her sleep at the age of just fifty. It was a terrible shock, particularly to George's father, David. Sarah had been twenty-five years younger than her husband and apparently in good health. George and Alice

travelled to Bideford for the funeral. They got on with each well enough but the loss of his mother deepened George's introspection and he became still more remote from Alice.

In late March George spent two weeks away at an excavation on the coast near Hornsea. With the arrival of spring Stephen Verrill reappeared in the garden at Boulby Cliff. Alice greeted him warmly and asked if he'd had a good holiday. He seemed happy enough and described briefly what he'd been up to since they'd last met. Stephen had a number of part time jobs in addition to his gardening work. He was employed in a carpenter's shop; he moved furniture and pianos from place to place; he occasionally served behind the bar at pubs in Whitby and Loftus.

During the first couple of days of the new season Stephen calculated his conversation and contact with Alice so as to encourage in her an increasing sense of confidence in him. To Stephen this was a kind of game. It was like stalking an animal: coaxing it, encouraging it, increasing its vulnerability until it found itself trapped and helpless. Then, when it was most defenceless, the shot, the kill…

On Thursday March 25th Stephen asked Alice about George's absence.
"Oh, George is away in Hornsea, working. He'll be back in a few days."
"Ah, I see. Nice, Hornsea. I did some woodworking at a house there a year or two ago."
"I've never been," she replied.
"I did see Mr Cromack, quite a few times actually, over Christmas and New Year, at a distance of course. Just happened to notice him in Whitby."
"Yes, he was working there for a while. He spends time in the library now and then."
"Oh. Must have been *after* work then, that I saw him."
Alice looked at Stephen, expecting more.
"Oh… no, just saying…"
He didn't offer any more information and Alice thought nothing

about it for a while, although her curiosity was a little piqued. What exactly was George doing after work? Alice had been under the impression that he always came straight home for dinner. She sensed that Stephen felt he'd unwittingly revealed something he shouldn't have. Of course, this was exactly the response that Stephen had planned to arouse in her. Alice felt compelled to request further details.

"Well, I was working in the Britannia in Whitby. I don't think Mr Cromack saw me. He was busy and I didn't want to interrupt."

"Busy? What, reading?"

"Well...no..."

"Was he alone?"

Silence. Then, "I don't think it's my place to gossip Ma'am. I'm sorry – I should just be doing the gardening. I've been talking out of turn."

The silence between them became charged.

Alice took a short, determined breath. "Was he with a woman?" Shaking her head a little, indignation rising.

Stephen feigned embarrassment, frowning, visibly unhappy, fiddling with the piece of woodwork he was preparing for the garden. "Well, yes. A young lady. I thought ..."

"Did they seem close?"

"Mrs Cromack, I wouldn't want to..."

"Please tell me, Stephen. I can see you're embarrassed but just spit it out please."

The irritation in her voice was sharp and clear and Stephen responded to it straight away.

"Well... Actually..." He drew it out, putting on a skilful performance, enticing Alice further into his sights. "They were holding hands, seemed fond of each other... and...", tipping his head and frowning more deeply, "...more..."

She was gone, running into the kitchen. Stephen was pleased with himself. That had gone pretty well.

At his next visit Stephen found himself alone in the garden. Alice did not come and greet him. That was to be expected, he thought. She felt vulnerable, abandoned by George, and because of his knowledge of events, emotionally exposed to Stephen. All part of the plan.

George returned home on Good Friday, April 2nd. Alice did not offer her routine kiss. Something was wrong. His heart began to sink. She was cleaning crockery, not looking at him.
"What's wrong?" he asked, feeling dread rising within him.
"Do you have something to tell me?"
"What do you mean, dear?"
She shook her head. "Don't play with me, George."
She'd found him out. How? He was done for. He sat at the table, silent for a while. Then, ashamed to the bottom of his soul, he told her everything. The Crocus, Jane, the clandestine coupling in York.
"It's over, Alice. I promise. I ended it three months ago, immediately after the site examination in York. Look, I can't apologise enough to you. I've treated you horribly."
Alice felt a part of her heart break away. She sat opposite him and allowed her tears to fall silently. George looked at her, then looked down at the table, lost.
"What's to be done?" he said.
"What do *you* want, George?"
"Oh God, that's just what *she* said." George began weeping too.
She reached across and took his hands. "Don't you love me any more?" Her tears caught in her voice.
"I do Alice! I do love you. I'm so sorry." He was beside himself.
"Then I forgive you," she said. George dropped his face to the table, his body shaking with sobs.

Relieved at the outcome of events and not wanting to open a can of worms, George did not ask Alice how she'd found out about him, and Alice did not volunteer Stephen as the source of the information.
When Stephen returned to the garden on the Wednesday after Easter he found George and Alice in good spirits and unusually warm with each other. He assumed that she had either not told

him what she knew, or that they'd resolved the issue between them. He was content in either case. If she'd kept the secret it would probably, in the fulness of time, infect their marriage. If they had resolved it and made up, Stephen would ensure that George's second fall would be all the more calamitous.

For some weeks all seemed well with the Cromacks and Stephen couldn't decide how to further his plans. The warm weather of summer arrived and the garden flourished. One afternoon, scheming over his ale in the Britannia, he had an inspired idea. The next day, sitting in his room in his brother's house in Loftus, he wrote a letter to Alice:

Whitby, Sunday, July 11th

Dear Mrs Cromack,

I have news which I fear may prove painful to you. I must tell you that some time ago your husband George deceived me. I accepted an offer of marriage from him and foolishly gave myself to him. He broke off our liaison when he had finished his pleasures with me and I have since come to understand that he is married already. Madam, I am with his child. I entrust myself to your mercy.

Out of shame I cannot reveal my name or my address to you but George will know how to find me.

Sadly,

A lost woman

Stephen did not know for sure exactly what had occurred between George and the girl, but he suspected that it had been an affair of some kind, whether consummated or not. The letter was a shot in the dark and a variety of outcomes were possible. It was a game in any case, and the letter could never be traced back to him as the Cromacks had never seen his handwriting. He posted it from Whitby in order to ensure the correct postmark, and waited for the results.

The envelope dropped through the letterbox at Boulby Cliff House on the morning of Tuesday July 13th. It knocked the wind out of Alice. She was mortified. George was at home and received the impact two minutes after his wife.

She was freely crying, wiping tears from her face. "George, is it true?"

He was stunned. George had heard nothing from Jane since their separation but, yes, it could be true. She could be six months pregnant by now.

Alice's despairing mind was tearing still more deeply into the situation. She had wanted children, as had George. Their absence was a real disappointment to them both. If Jane had become pregnant it meant that it was she, Alice who was the impediment to the creation of a family. If that was so how could she stand in George's way now? Surely she must withdraw. She felt that her life had suddenly fallen to pieces.

George was speaking. "Alice, I'll go and find her now. Then we'll know if this is true."

"Yes. Go now please. Get it over with," she replied.

George walked up to the main road and caught the bus to Boulby station, meeting the connection to Whitby from there. He made his way straight to the Crocus tea room. Jane was gone. She'd left her job in January, probably fearing to meet George again, and had provided no forwarding address. The shop had since changed proprietors and there was no remaining record of Jane's home address. He was at a loss.

Sitting on a bench in the street George felt the turmoil within himself. He thought hard but no solution came to him. It seemed that the only available option was to search the streets for her. For all he knew she could have moved far away.

In his mind he analysed the letter. It did not ring true to him. There were several lies in it that he could not square with Jane's character. He had *not* asked her to marry him, he had *not* hidden his own marriage from her, and the description of his selfish abuse of her was cruel and surely inaccurate. But how could he prove any of this to Alice without Jane herself to verify it? Indeed, how well had he come to know Jane? In the brief time they spent together he'd felt that their souls were very close, but had he naïvely deluded himself?

The letter claimed that he would know how to find her. But considering she'd quit her job six months ago and had never told him her home address how did she think he was to go about that? The only reasoning George could find was that she hadn't anticipated the shop would change hands, trusting that he'd be able to trace her from there. But it was clear that no such action was possible.

He returned to Alice and threw up his hands. "I don't know. How can I know?"

"George, if she is pregnant with your child you must find her. And if you can have a family with her…then we must end."

"Alice, please…"

"No George, I can't go on like this. You'll need to find out."

Alice moved George's clothes into the second bedroom. It effectively marked the end of their marriage.

Stephen Verrill could never have imagined that his deception would achieve such an effective outcome.

Stephen arrived at Boulby Cliff for work the day after the letter's arrival. Something was clearly going on between George and Alice. Neither of them came out of the house to greet him all day, and he heard them talking, often with some urgency. He put two and two together and found himself smiling, nostrils flaring, as he occupied himself. Things were going his way. He could smell his quarry's scent. The anticipation was exquisite.

On Thursday morning Stephen saw George leave, clutching a suitcase. Alice remained indoors. He caught the sound of her crying on several occasions.

In the afternoon he put his head round the back door. There she was, at the table, face drenched in tears.

"Oh, Mrs Cromack," he said, feigning surprise. "What's to be done? Can I help?"

"No Stephen. I'm sorry, please leave me alone." She sniffed, walked over, and muttering an apology, shut him out.

George took a room in Whitby and did all he could to find Jane in

order to determine the veracity of the letter. As it turned out, he could achieve little, and he morbidly found himself in the Britannia on Saturday night, drinking alone. He looked up and there was Stephen, standing by the table.
"Hope I'm not intruding Mr George."
George was a little startled. "Stephen! No, not at all."
Stephen settled himself on the opposite bench. "I hope everything's alright at the house?"
"Er... well... We're trying to sort out a few things. Nothing serious. I'm spending a few days here in town."
"Ah. Work, I expect?"
"Hm..."
George was clearly preoccupied and not in the mood for a conversation.
"I'll leave you to it then Mr George. See you next week."
"Well... maybe..."

On Monday morning, July 19th, Alice opened the kitchen door and was surprised to find Stephen at work, shirtless, towards the bottom of the garden. Monday was not normally one his days. She walked halfway along the path and called, "I didn't expect to see you today Stephen."
"I had some things to finish, Mrs Alice," he called back. "I hope you don't mind."
"No of course not. I'll bring you a brew."
The tea was duly brought. Alice stood, holding her cup. Stephen placed his mug carefully on the ground beside him.
"I saw Mr George in Whitby on Saturday night." Stephen looked down, pretending to concentrate on his work.
"Ah. All well?"
"Aye. In the Britannia. Never seen him so happy!" With a little chuckle.
"Happy?" said Alice.
"Oh aye! He can be the life and soul of the party. He was still drinking when I left at eleven or thereabouts."
"Happy...?" She walked back to the kitchen in confusion.

"Shan't be long now…" muttered Stephen to himself.
The endgame, he thought. The King was absent. The Queen was almost cornered.

Stephen made his next move on Wednesday. He asked Alice if George had returned. She seemed distant and upset. No, she wasn't expecting him back for a while. Stephen led her to believe that George had been in the Britannia again the previous night.
"Drinking with his mates again?" she asked, acidly.
"No. No…"
She sighed. "Tell me then…?"
"Well…"
Alice was silent, waiting for details. "Stephen, for God's sake…"
"I'd rather not Mrs George. If you don't mind. I don't want to bring trouble."
The situation was precarious but Stephen felt the clockwork of his scheming click into final alignment. If George appeared Stephen's lies would be exposed, but his excitement made him reckless.
Alice squatted close to him and spoke with insistence. "Stephen, I think you're my friend. Please tell me."
Her plea delighted him but he withheld himself, drawing out the intoxication of the trap still further. He looked askance at her, shaking his head. "Please Alice…"
Stephen's unexpected and subdued use of her Christian name, without the usual missus, shocked Alice a little and she felt suddenly exposed and fearful. Saying nothing more she rose and walked back along the path and into the house.
Ten minutes later she was back. She'd been crying.
"Tell me, dammit!"
He stood up, turned to her, sighed and said, "Alice, he had a woman with him." He paused and looked directly at her, faking reluctance. "She was…" – he gestured *pregnant* with his hands – "I think it might have been…"
But she was sobbing out loud before he could finish. He reached out and took her in his arms. She allowed him to do so, and col-

lapsed in what she thought was his consolation. Her arms clasped around him and he drew her close, stroking her gently. He pressed his nose into her hair, and as he did so caught sight of George standing at the side of the house. Alice was as yet unaware of his presence and Stephen allowed his embrace of her to become more encouraging, possessive. Unintentionally she found herself responding to it, mistaking it for affection. She pushed her body into his and would have kissed him had she not at that moment sensed George's eyes on her. She froze.

George spoke quietly but with an anguished bitterness. "How could you? How *could* you!?"

She broke away from Stephen. "George?" she muttered in confusion.

Maintaining the steely ice of his stare, George shook his head almost imperceptibly. He retraced his steps around the side of the house and was gone. Alice ran after him as far as the garden gate, calling him back, but George was filled with a red rage. It was over. Alice was weeping on her knees by the front gate. Stephen appeared by her side, knelt and cradled her in his arms, telling her he was sorry. In a while the outermost layers of her despair withdrew and she knelt there in silence, broken, face wet, looking at the ground.

"Mrs... Alice," he said. I think I should go. I'll come back in a day or two and collect my things."

Her face remained downcast but she nodded yes, and Stephen was gone.

Friday July 23rd, 1915

On Friday morning Alice received a brief note in the mail from George. He informed her that he'd enlisted in the army and was leaving the area to commence his basic training. He expected to join the fight in Flanders in a month or two. He would maintain the lease on Boulby Cliff House until she informed him that it was no longer required or until their marriage was dissolved. It was a terse, loveless communication. Her sorrow caught in her throat –

today should have been their fifth wedding anniversary.

Stephen arrived at the house a few minutes after noon. He wandered around the garden for a while, making a show of collecting his things, expecting that she was watching him. After a short while he went and tapped on the back door. Alice was sitting at the kitchen table. She looked drained and pale, helpless. She didn't look up. She was crushed, her life shattered, destroyed, worthless.

It was time. Stephen pulled a chair close to her and sat down. He put one hand on her arm. With the other he stroked her lips and brushed her face. Then she looked at him and knew. She heard the stillness of the house, the singing of the garden birds, the soft buzz of the honey bees, the summer breeze high up in the trees around the house, the distant wash of the sea. She felt her isolation very keenly and saw the strength in his arms and the intention in his eyes, no longer the eyes of a boy.

There was no fight in her. Easier to just allow it to happen.

19. ROSE

Wednesday December 8th – Thursday December 9th, 1965

Rose, thrilled and realising that the body had become conscious, crouched down on all fours and peered closely into the newly open eyes. "Hello my love."
There was no answer. The woman's eyes were fixed on Rose and seemed to follow her movements but the face remained impassive and the body remained inert. The faint scent was unchanged. Rose gently felt for further signs of life but there was neither pulse nor heartbeat, and she didn't appear to be breathing.
Rose returned to her wooden stool and looked down.
"What's your name my dear?"
No answer of course, just the eyes, watching.
"I'll call you Jill. I'm Rose. Welcome home."
No response.
"I wonder how long you've been in the ground…"
Rose chatted to Jill for most of the night. First she explained how she'd uncovered Jill's bones after the collapse of the cliff and the ruin of the garden wall. Then she told Jill as much as she knew about her family history, working backwards from her mother dying the previous year, then how the four of them had moved into Boulby Cliff forty-two years previously. Her early life on Cappleman Farm. Then the stories from before her birth – young Moll, Margery, Mother Abigail and the great, mysterious Kate.
With a start Rose realised it was nearly 4am. She was astonished that she'd been able to fill such a tract of time with stories about her own family, with (as far as she remembered) no repetition.
Jill had remained immobile, and except for the small glow of consciousness in her eyes, apparently dead throughout. As far as Rose was aware there had been no further change in the body. It looked as if it might have been recently pulled out of a bog and allowed to dry.

"I'm away to bed, Jill my love. Pleasant dreams. I'll see you in the morning." Then, as an afterthought: "Don't do anything I wouldn't do."

On the way back to the house she caught herself laughing softly at her own humour – a very rare occurrence for her.

The next morning Rose was in the shed by 8.45, yawning. The paraffin heater had burned out but there was still a little warmth in the hut. Rose refilled and lit it, said hello to Jill and sat down. At first overcast and dark, the sky brightened as the sun rose higher and a dull daylight soon illuminated the potting shed. Rose squatted down and inspected Jill's face. No change as far as she could see. She put her fingers to Jill's lips. No sign of breathing. The pressure of her fingers was insufficient to part the lips themselves. The flesh seemed hard and fixed, still somewhat mummified. A little delicate prodding elsewhere revealed the same unyielding texture. Only the outer layers of skin seemed to have any suppleness at all. The frame inside remained rigid.

Rose moved her fingers to within an inch or so of Jill's eyes. The lids blinked, seemingly in reflex. Rose sat back on her heels. "Well that's a relief m'dear. I was starting to think I'd imagined it."

Other than that single blink there was no movement all morning, and Rose was unaware of any further improvement in Jill's physical condition.

In the early afternoon, just after lunch, Jimmy Jackson delivered a box of groceries and foodstuffs in preparation for Christmas. It was the first of two deliveries she'd scheduled that December. Jimmy had been a Yorkshire farmer all his life and had inherited the business from his father. As was the case with Tommy the postman, Rose occasionally spoke a few words with Jimmy at the door. He was "Jimmy", she was "Miss Headlam."

Rose was "Rose" to nobody.

It occurred to her that Jill probably didn't even know what time of year it was, so she returned to the potting shed and told her about the delivery of Christmas goods. Rose wasn't a particularly religious person and had rarely been to church but she did enjoy listening to the broadcast carol service from King's College every

Christmas Eve.

Rose thought that Jill might be interested in the recent terrible weather, so she recounted the details of that too, along with all the travel disruption horror stories she'd heard reported on the radio. She also explained that, although she wasn't a sociable type, she did know a few local people a bit. Tommy Widdop the postman; Jimmy Jackson the farmer...

At the mention of Jimmy's name Rose thought she detected a very slight inclination of Jill's head and a wider opening of the eyelids, giving the impression that some detail of Rose's conversation had caught Jill's attention. Rose stopped talking and instantly crouched down to have a closer look.

"Jimmy," she said, partly to herself. There was no further movement but Rose was sure that some small change had indeed occurred. She nodded her head shallowly. "I think – you knew Jimmy Jackson..."

20. ALICE AND STEPHEN
Friday July 23rd – Tuesday October 26th, 1915

The culmination of Stephen's strategy was emotionless and impersonal, its physical execution requiring just a few minutes, although he shouted in incoherent self-congratulation at the moment of its ultimate realisation.

When it was over he got dressed and went downstairs into the garden where he walked about, hands in pockets, in quiet celebration. He rolled himself a smoke. Stephen felt at peace, the chase over, his victory won. He smiled at himself in contentment, much as a hunter of big game might feel when contemplating the slain prize. It had been rather like receiving a much desired birthday present – the long wait over, the package delivered at last, the unwrapping.

Alice lay alone, broken and lost, unable to find herself. She didn't know who she was – if she was anyone. She didn't cry but lay on her side, eyes wide open, trying to locate some inner landscape that she recognised, but found nothing. She'd watched what had happened from a point far away, up beyond the room. There had been a man and a doll. She didn't recognise the doll and saw only the back of the man's head.

The house was quiet and still.

At about quarter past two Stephen came in from the garden, took off his clothes in the kitchen and went up to her again.

It was extraordinarily warm that day and the garden submitted to the blaze. The flowers spread their vivid uncaring faces to the sky, the tight buds opening to the penetrative heat of the sun. The overnight rain had encouraged the slugs and snails out of their hiding places and their slimy trails were visible throughout the grounds. The trees dripped the sticky dew of aphids, and the round fruits beneath the leafy canopies remained slippery with rainwater. The excited honey bees were engrossed in their instinctive task, the hive thrumming with their exertions, and the butterflies and bumble bees danced among the blooms and bushes. The stonework of the house shimmered in the day's heat but the interior remained comfortably cool.

Three o'clock found Stephen back in the kitchen. He put the kettle on, made two mugs of tea and took one up to Alice. She was lying on her side once more, motionless.

"I made you some char," he said. "Cheer up," rubbing his hand on her shoulder. Then he was gone.

Alice lay there for over an hour, then sat up and drank the tea cold. She perched on the edge of the bed, feet on the floor for some time before getting dressed.

Stephen was sitting quietly at the table when she appeared. He said nothing and she couldn't look at him. It was nearly half past four. The afternoon was still warm and the birds were still singing. She went to the larder and took out some bread, cheese, butter and jam, placing the food on the kitchen table. Then she fetched plates and cutlery and sat down opposite him. No words were spoken and neither of them ate, but after a short pause he reached out and covered her hand with his. Alice knew he was looking at her but was unable to raise her own gaze more than an inch or two. Stephen gently stroked the back of her hand. The gesture wasn't entirely devoid of affection.

Without making any request or suggestion, Stephen moved into Boulby Cliff House with Alice. He continued to fiddle in the garden and kept up his employment behind the bar at Whitby. He shelved the heavier jobs, the furniture moving, woodworking and the like, preferring to spend time in his new home. Alice rarely said much and never smiled. That didn't concern Stephen. She cooked for him, prepared his clothes and continued to keep the house in order. With only rare exceptions he treated her like an automaton and her deep sense of self-worthlessness allowed him to do so. Having nowhere to go, and there being no one to whom she felt able to turn, Alice effectively became his wife and Stephen took from her all the usual manifestations of marital entertainment.

Alice no longer sang.

On the morning of Tuesday August 10th Stephen intercepted a letter addressed to Alice. He'd anticipated that George might try to contact her so he locked himself in the outhouse and read it:

Coltersdale, Masham
Sunday, August 8th

My Darling Alice,

I have been sick with remorse since I last saw you. I behaved so appallingly and ran off without giving you any chance to explain what was happening. How can you ever forgive me?
I am now committed to training here in the camp but I hope to have word from you. My heart is so full of regret for all the wrong I've done you. I am on my knees and begging your forgiveness. Please look kindly on me. If you send me word I'll come home to you when I have leave. You can write to me here at Coltersdale.

Your Love,

George

Stephen burnt the letter.

George never appeared at the house. Stephen guessed that, having received no reply from Alice, George had resigned himself to the fact that she was finished with him.

After a couple of months Stephen began to get bored, as he always did. The cruelty he had brought to all his previous relationships with the opposite sex began to creep into this one too. He began to call Alice names, telling her she was stupid, slow, dense. He began to push her around physically and was soon hitting her, often in response to trivial things. Alice took the abuse. She felt worthless, ashamed, and thought she deserved no better.

One day in early September Doris Naseby came knocking at the door. Alice opened it but Stephen was next to her in a flash. Doris stepped back in amazement.

"Stephen?"

"'allo Mrs Naseby. Nice to see you. Bet you didn't expect to see me 'ere."

To Alice she said, "Is everything all right?"

Before Alice could answer, Stephen said, "It is, thank you – Doris." He mocked her with an emphasised D. "Things have moved on 'ere, as you can see."

"I heard George had gone. What happened?" asked Doris.

"He's buggered off to war and left 'er. *We're* together now, she and me – and very 'appy, thank you. Your presence is not required. Tarra." And he shut the door in her face.

Stephen would boast to his drinking buddies about his successful conquest of his employer's wife. He described how Cromack had uprooted himself and left her in favour of a life of military excitement. How she had, understandably, looked to Stephen himself for the protection and support of a strong man. For the entertainment of his friends he made up stories involving Alice that were grotesque and untrue.

Alice felt almost nothing. The light in her life had gone out and the world was suddenly very dark. It seemed to her that her soul had fled with all her love and had given her up as a lost cause.

Stephen intercepted a second letter from George on Friday, September 24th.

Artois, Friday September 17th

My Dear Darling Alice,

I am at the front line and have been in action. It is a frightful place and I fear we may never meet again. You haven't replied to the letter I sent from Coltersdale and I am very frightened that you have given up on me. I will love you for ever my beautiful Alice, and implore your forgiveness with all my heart. Please write to me by return – even a short note, reassuring me that all is not lost between us.

My tears fall on this paper as I write. I'm yours, my Dear Love,

George

Stephen tore it up and burnt the bits.

As the weeks passed Alice slowly began to emerge from her despair. The first thing she felt as her emotions regrew was a deep hatred for Stephen. She tried to refuse his attentions but he was always able to overcome her with his strength. In fact he enjoyed punching her into submission.

Alice was heartbroken that George hadn't tried to contact her. Deciding to take the initiative she wrote to him herself:

Boulby Cliff House, Monday, October 4th

My dear husband George,

I hope very much that this letter will find you. I do not know where you are so I'm sending this via your father. I want us to forget the terrible things that have happened between us and start our lives again. I miss so much the happiness of our early days. I know you must think badly of me – and I have terrible things to tell you – that you <u>must</u> know.
Please, George, my Love. Think of me, wherever you are. Try to forgive me – <u>I will need all your forgiveness.</u>

I am still yours,

Alice

She sealed it in an envelope and wrote a note to George's father asking him to please forward the enclosure. Sealing both items in a second envelope, she addressed the package to Mr David Cromack at his address in Bideford, North Devon.

Not expecting Stephen to return to the house until later in the evening Alice set out to walk the mile to the post box on the main road. As luck would have it she met Stephen coming in the opposite direction.

"Where d'ya think you're goin'?" he asked.

"For a walk," she replied coolly.

Stephen had other ideas, and gripping her arm in his hand said, "Don't think so." He began to forcefully drag her back along the lane, the aggressive action dislodging the letter she was holding in her pocket. It fell to the ground and he picked it up.

"What's this then?" Releasing her, he tore it open and read it on the spot. She thought of trying to run but knew he'd catch her easily, and the punishment for such an attempt would amplify the thrashing that already awaited her.

Stephen said nothing, but screwed up the letter and put it in his pocket. He looked at her coldly, reached out and took hold of her hair, then led her back to the house. She cried out several times as he pulled her behind him, demanding to be released, but his boot silenced her on each occasion. He hurled her through the front door and slammed it shut behind him. Alice lay cowering on the floor, dreading what was to come. Stephen removed his belt and beat her, thoroughly and at length. It took two weeks for the contusions to heal.

When she'd more or less fully recovered and was able to walk again without pain Alice decided to seek refuge with the Nasebys. She didn't know them very well but they seemed kind people. Stephen had adopted the trick of giving Alice false information about his absence from the house. He would for example tell her that he'd be home at eleven in the evening, but then return at six thirty. Or he'd say he was going out for a couple of hours only to reappear twenty minutes later. She could never be sure. If he caught her trying to make trouble he would beat her, and she was very frightened of him.

On Friday October 22nd, when Stephen had been absent for most of the morning, Alice took her life in her hands and walked for more than a mile up the lane to the Naseby's house. It was a mild day for October. The house appeared shut up. She knocked several times at the door and walked around the grounds trying to find someone in whom she might confide. The window shutters were all closed and there was no one home. Alice made her way back to Boulby Cliff full of disappointment and anxiety. She opened the front door and there he was, waiting for her.

"Where've you been?"

Her head sank as she felt the inevitable punishment approaching.

"I went up the road to see Doris."

"What for?"

She didn't answer but looked dully at him. She knew he was going to beat her close to death.

"Why'd you come back?"

She hung her head, resigned to her fate. "There was nobody there…"

He sighed. "Don't do that again. Please." His manner was more subdued than usual and Alice thought she detected something more gentle in him than the accustomed mocking cruelty. She was surprised. There was no beating, and his nocturnal employment of her was less brutal than it usually was.

Afterwards she lay quietly for a while on her back in the darkness of the bedroom. Stephen had turned away from her onto his side but she sensed that he wasn't asleep. Something had happened. Alice's natural kindness found an opportunity to show itself – turning towards him she reached out and rested her hand on his arm, feeling him flinch with surprise. He turned his head a little, listening.

"What's wrong?" she asked quietly.

There was silence for a while. Owls hooted in the stillness.

"My dad died."

Her eyes moistened with tears of sympathy, remembering her own father, the bakery, the happy life she'd shared with him. Alice moved close to Stephen, pressed her body against his and put both her arms round him. He wasn't expecting that and tensed in response, though quickly relaxed and permitted her embrace. She felt warm, comforting.

"I'm Sorry Stephen."

"'S'all right. I didn't know 'im. He walked out on us when I was seven. I never saw him again."

She was quiet. Then, "But you only get one father."

He was quiet for a while. "How did you know?"

"I felt it in you. In the way you…"

He turned so they were face to face in the dark and began to brush her body gently with his fingers. Her arms remained around him, pulling him close.

"You were sad," she whispered. She could just make out his eyes shining in the dark.

He murmured, "I thought maybe 'e'd come back one day…"

His sorrowed softened her heart. She kissed him on the lips – something she'd never yet willingly done.

Stephen was surprised. He returned her kiss.

The physical act that followed, full of compassion and tenderness, was very new to Stephen. Afterwards, as Alice slept, he lay awake trying to come to terms with what had just happened. He found himself increasingly disturbed by it, and as the light of dawn appeared he rose, dressed and walked to Boulby Station. Catching the early train to Whitby he dossed about all day and was completely drunk by lunchtime. The binge went on and he stayed away from the house for several days.

Alice thought he was gone for good, but in the fulness of time, and having banished any possibility of feeling more than contempt for Alice, he turned up again and was his old, cruel self. The single moment of love between them (if that is what it was) was crushed like an unwanted flower. Alice again became no more than a thing to Stephen and he turned his imagination to finding new ways to torture her.

21. Friday December 10th, 1965

In the darkest silence of the night, while Rose was asleep in bed, the latch on the potting shed door was released from the inside, giving a little click as it lifted. The door swung slowly open under its own weight.

Rose awoke at 8am, got dressed and made her way down to the kitchen for breakfast. She set the kettle to boil and prepared herself some toast. The radio news announced that a fireball had been seen the previous afternoon, streaking across the skies of Ontario, Michigan and Ohio. There were reports of an object having crashed near a small town in Pennsylvania. Rose found herself wondering if the Doctor and his companions would arrive to investigate it. *Thunderball*, the fourth James Bond movie, had premiered in Tokyo.

She sat at the table and reached for the butter. The room darkened slightly and Rose sensed movement. She turned and looked towards the window in the kitchen door. Someone was standing just outside. A dark figure.

"Oh my goodness..." she said.

Rose stood, unlocked the door and swung it open slowly. She knew who it would be, and there she was. Jill was standing upright, motionless in the light of the morning, having made her way from the potting shed along the path to the back door. She was impassive, dark, and appeared to all intents and purposes to be a corpse, fixed in place and blocking the door like an inconveniently delivered garden statue.

"Welcome, my love," said Rose. "You are very welcome here."

Jill displayed no movement or response. Rose held out both her hands and concentrated hard on Jill's eyes, still gleaming with awareness. "Come inside," she whispered. Jill slowly raised both her forearms and allowed Rose to take her hands. They felt papery and fragile. Rose stepped carefully backwards into the kitchen. Jill followed step by step. When she was able Rose closed the door and walked around her new companion, touching her body here and there, assessing its condition. Jill felt leathery and dry but there was some new resilience in the flesh. Rose stood before her and took Jill's upper arms in her hands in a partial embrace. Now that Jill was standing straight the details of her torso could more clearly be seen. Looking down, Rose saw that Jill's abdomen was split across from side to side. Within the split there seemed to be four substantial puncture wounds arranged in a horizontal line. Rose investigated them more deeply with her fingers, Jill offering no resistance or complaint. The holes were uniform and equally separated.

"Oh my... You poor, poor love," she said, and began to cry a little. "Whatever happened to you?"

22. STEPHEN AND ALICE

Saturday December 4th, 1915, 9.30pm

In his mind, Stephen had formulated new ways in which he could continue to entertain himself with Alice. His fantasies involved humiliating and further degrading her, crushing her ever smaller. One or two of his mental images involved bringing his drinking buddies home and "introducing" them to her. The prospect of such things fuelled his viciousness and filled him with glee.

On Saturday December 4th Stephen was at the pub with his friends in Boulby. On occasions like this he would often stay away from the house until well after midnight, staggering home in the small hours before passing out downstairs. On a couple of occasions Alice had to clean up his vomit in the morning.

This evening she used his absence as an opportunity to bathe. She put several pitchers on the range to heat the water and collected the tin bath from its nail on the wall in the outhouse. It took about half an hour to fill the tub sufficiently. She poured soap shavings into the water, gathered some towels, removed her clothes and stepped in. Despite the miserable, loveless circumstances in which she now lived, Alice enjoyed the warm water and began to relax.

A few minutes later she heard boots approaching along the front path, then a key turning in the lock. He was back early.

"Alice!" It was Stephen, calling.

"I'm in the bath. Give me a few minutes please?"

A pause. Then, "In the bath, eh?" She heard subdued laughter beyond the door, from several voices, and was instantly very frightened.

Stephen had planned on making Alice suffer tonight with one of his twisted ideas, and had brought his friends with him so they could become part of his entertainment, but he hadn't anticipated this extra opportunity for cruelty.

"I'll be there in a minute," she said, trying to cover the trembling in her voice.

Stephen pushed the door ajar and peered round it. "Don't trouble yourself love." He pushed the door fully open and walked in, beckoning to his companions. Gilbert Rathmell, Albin Thackrey and Bill Greenwood entered the kitchen. Alice sank into the water as fully as she could and tried to cover herself with her arms and hands. Her heart was beating wildly. "Please leave," she said, "you're frightening me." Her lips were quivering and she couldn't form the words clearly.

Bill, older than the others, was clearly embarrassed, his breathing audible, passing his rolled up cap between his hands, looking from side to side, trying to keep Alice out of his line of sight. Gilbert and Albin stared fixedly at her, trying to penetrate the water with their gaze.

"No, I think we'll stay," said Stephen. "I think you ought to entertain my friends. Stand up."

Horrified, she shook her head *no*.

Bill said, "Stephen, enough…"

"No," said Stephen, holding up his hand to Bill in a negative gesture. "She'll do as she's told. Up you get Alice." Then, murmuring, "Let's all 'ave a look at you."

Alice was terrified and began to cry. She looked at Bill, pleading with her eyes.

Then things happened very fast. Stephen took a threatening step toward her, clenched his fist and shouted, "STAND UP!" But even before the command had been issued Alice uncovered herself, bathwater spattering noisily on the kitchen floor, and began to stand. In the same second Bill lunged forward. He shouted, "For God's sake, Verrill!", grabbed Stephen's arm and punched him hard in the face. To Gilbert and Albin he shouted, "You two get out of here before I beat the shite out of you!" They were gone instantly. Alice splashed back down and tried to hide herself in what remained of the water. Bill spoke directly to her, head shaking. "I'm very sorry." He grabbed Stephen by the arm, opened the back door and pushed him out into the night. Alice heard him say, "And you, you evil bastard!..."

Bill closed the back door behind him and walked toward Stephen, who stared at him with fright and amazement, suddenly defenceless in the face of a bigger man. Filled with disgust and fury, Bill took his fists and boots to Stephen. He beat him to within an inch of his life, allowing his overwhelming anger to subside only when his opponent lay before him, bloodied and almost unconscious.

Alice cowered, terror-struck, in the puddle of cooling bathwater, listening to the sustained violence outside. A moment of silence followed the onslaught, then the back door opened. She instinctively made herself as small as possible in the water. Bill's head appeared round the door. "You should come with me," he said. Alice shook her head vigorously. "It'll be safer. I think you should get dressed and let me take you away from here."

"No," mumbled Alice, reinforcing the negative with a tiny headshake. She was confused and didn't know what to do. Maybe she should go...?

"Then lock yourself in and let him sober up overnight in the privy. It won't do the bastard any harm. Keep yourself safe inside till morning – *and don't let him in.*" He shut the door but immediately opened it again. "If he makes trouble for you, you find me in the village. I'm Bill – Bill Greenwood. Remember."

She nodded and said, "Thank you," choking on the words,

Bill withdrew, shutting the kitchen door behind him. The next second Alice heard him addressing Stephen. "If you take a hand to that woman – if I hear you've abused her *IN ANY WAY*," (there was the sound of a savage kick), "I will *kill* you. Do you understand?" (two hard kicks). "Say yes, you *fuck*in' *gob*shite *worth*less *arse*hole!" (all accompanied by rhythmic bootings). There were whimpers and pleading mewls, followed by a final, brutal kick. Then Bill was gone, passing by the side of the house, along the front path and away into the road.

In the dead silence that followed Alice rose from the bath, quickly dried and dressed herself. She put on her coat and opened the back door. It was a cold night, clear and starlit. The moon showed a narrow crescent. Stephen was lying on the ground as if he'd decided to give up living. There was enough light for her to see that he'd taken a serious beating. In the morning he'd be a mass of swellings and bruises. She knelt beside him and put her hand on his arm.

Stephen was drunk, humiliated and in no mood for kindness. He opened his eyes and spat venomous abuse at her. Alice withdrew her contact and stood. A moment later Stephen was upright, wincing with pain as he tried to steady himself on his feet.

"You bitch! You show me up in front of me mates?" He lunged at her and she backed away. But Stephen was determined, and grabbing the sleeve of her coat shook her hard. Alice responded by allowing the coat to slide off her. He spat, "I'll teach you, tart! You won't be doin' that again."

Stephen was lunging out and striking her with his fists. Alice backed away as well as she could, hands raised in defence. She turned and ran along the garden path to the potting shed. Stephen's injuries meant that he moved more slowly than she. Alice knew what she needed. She opened the potting shed door and picked up the hammer she remembered was on the table inside. Turning quickly she met Stephen, almost on top of her. She swung the hammer sideways and caught him on the arm. Stephen howled in pain and wheeled aside. Alice tried to run away from him toward the house but he caught her arm and spun her round to face him. She raised the hammer above her head and would have delivered a considerable blow with it but Stephen was too quick for her. There was a garden fork leaning by the side of the potting shed. In his rage he picked the tool up, levelled it, and drove the four tines through Alice's abdomen. The force of it briefly lifted her a couple of inches off the ground. Alice stopped all movement. She dropped the hammer and looked down at herself for a moment, then fell, her body slipping free of the fork as she did so.

Stephen was horrified. He hadn't intended things to go this far. Alice was still alive and soundlessly pleading for her life from where she lay, a great deal of dark blood pooling around her. There was no way back. He picked up the hammer and struck her with all his force, smashing in the left side of her head. She was immediately still.

In the clear, starry cold Stephen surveyed his work. He dropped the bloody hammer and looked around him, checking that he was indeed alone. What next? Drop the body over the cliff. No, it would be washed up and discovered – and the wounds from the garden fork would indicate murder rather than an accident. He quickly decided what had to be done.

As the night wore on Stephen dug a grave for Alice. It was a long job but the preceding weeks had been very wet and the earth was not too tightly packed. He had little difficulty in digging down to a depth of more than four feet in the earth beyond the strawberry bed at the northeast edge of the garden. He took hold of Alice's body by the ankles, dragged her along the path, tipped her into the hole and filled in the grave. No one would ever know.

When the job was done he filled two of Alice's metal pitchers with water and washed away her blood as best he could. The coming rain would do the rest. He returned to the house, emptied Alice's bath and prepared one for himself. Later he sat silently at the kitchen table, eyes staring ahead.

23. STEPHEN

Sunday December 5th, 1915 – Thursday February 10th, 1916

Stephen plotted his actions carefully over the following few months. The suddenness of Alice's death shocked and haunted him although he felt no remorse for it. She'd brought it on herself by attacking him, after all, but Stephen knew that what he'd done would be viewed as murder in the eyes of the law. If caught he would almost certainly hang. So – he mustn't be caught.

He continued to live in the house, making an effort to greet the few visitors personally at the door – the postman, Albert Jackson and the other folk who occasionally made deliveries. He wanted to give the impression of continued normality. They'd all become used to the idea of Alice and Stephen by now and so they would, he hoped, not suspect that anything was wrong. Now and then one of them asked after her and Stephen would tell them that she was very well but hadn't woken up yet, was in the bath, was visiting friends, or some such. He systematically burnt all her possessions – her clothing piece by piece and all her personal things – making sure that everything was completely destroyed. Stephen had initially decided to allow George's belongings to remain in the house – his clothes, books, papers and other items – but during his programme of destruction he decided to get rid of all those things too. If George ever came back to the house he'd find it empty and assume that Alice had got rid of all his stuff. The thought amused Stephen greatly. He burned everything, although he inspected each of their photographs prior to execution. George with his parents; Alice with her father; an old photograph showing Alice's father with an unknown woman, probably her mother. The wedding photographs they'd had taken in 1910 were the last to be committed to the flames. Stephen left only the furniture and the kitchenware – and that remained only because he continued to use it.

He took up his furniture-moving and woodworking again and maintained his association with his friends – except for Bill, who scowled at him from a distance. His conversation still included mention of Alice as if she were alive although his fabricated filthy stories about her ceased. Albin, Gilbert and the others tacitly took Stephen's discontinuance of the stories to be the result of Bill's punishment of him that Saturday night at Boulby Cliff.

For Christmas and the New Year he and has elder brother Robert travelled to London and spent the festive season with their mother in the house where they'd both been born. Margaret (larger than life in every way and known as Peggy to her friends) was a popular East End character. By Christmas 1915 she was sixty years old and lived alone. No one mourned Clifford Verrill, her recently deceased ex-husband, who'd been found hung from a tree in Epping Forest, circumstances unknown. He'd run off with a neighbour's daughter in 1903 when the boys were eleven and seven years old and they'd never seen him again. Peggy subsequently rejected the name Verrill and resumed the use of her maiden name. Everyone knew her as Peggy Black.

As the year passed to 1916 there was some talk in the streets about compulsory war service in the army. Soon, a bill would be brought before parliament. Stephen was not keen on the idea of enforced military service, though his brother appeared to welcome the news.

They returned to Yorkshire a few days after New Year and Stephen made his way back to the house. It was cold and empty, undisturbed, although there was another letter from George. Stephen opened it and found it be the usual pleading noise, asking for forgiveness and keening after Alice's love. All pointless now. It went the way of the letters that had preceded it. The envelopes continued to arrive throughout January and into February. They all went into the flames, unopened.

Stephen knew what he had to do next. In early February he wrote to Bill Hardaker and told him that he no longer required the lease on Boulby Cliff House. He and Alice would be emigrating to Canada. He wrote to his mother and brother with the news that he'd accepted a job in North America (he was not specific about the precise locality or nature of the work). He and his "girl" planned to move away immediately. He gave the same loose outline to his various friends and work mates, telling them that he was "under orders" not to divulge his future whereabouts or activities.

The day before Stephen left the house for the last time he walked to the bottom of the garden and stood by Alice's grave. A crisp wind blew in from the sea. As he looked down at the cold earth he remembered the warmth of that night with her – the night after he'd received the telegram informing him of his father's death – and felt a chasm of emptiness in his soul.

On Thursday February 10th, 1916, having gathered together his few belongings in a bag, he travelled to Ireland, the one part of the British Isles exempted from the forthcoming Military Service Act, and kept his head down for the remainder of the war.

24

Friday December 10th, 1965

Jill seemed unable to move inside the house without Rose's assistance, always with their hands clasped and step by step, as with her initial entry via the kitchen door. It took some time but Rose eventually managed to manoeuvre her into the sitting room. She turned on the electric fire and invited Jill to be seated. Jill remained standing, giving no indication that she had understood the invitation.

"I'll get you something to wear," said Rose and ran upstairs. Less than a minute later she was back with a dressing gown which she draped around Jill. The effect was ridiculous, like dressing a hat stand. Rose was able to slide one of Jill's arms into one of the sleeves but couldn't manage the other one. Jill was taller than she and her body was stiff. Rose was frightened she might actually break off Jill's arm if she tried to bend it into the sleeve, so the dressing gown remained only partly in place. She could at least secure it in front with the tie belt.

Standing back to survey her efforts Rose found the spectacle absurd and could not suppress a small laugh. Jill's eyes followed her but otherwise there was no movement.

"Jill, love. My house is your house. Sit, stand, move about as you please."

Rose sat and tried to plan what to do next. A few possibilities presented themselves and she made some notes. At lunchtime she prepared some soup and held a spoonful close to Jill's face. There was no response, the mouth remaining hard and sealed. Rose touched the spoon to the lips and tipped gently. The liquid came dribbling down Jill's chin. Rose set the spoon and bowl on the table and cleaned the spillage away.

"Sorry about that m'dear. I guess we'll just have to take things one step at a time."

Rose pottered about for the rest of the day. She made jam tarts in the kitchen and listened to the radio, all the while trying to work out how to go forward with Jill. She spoke to her throughout the day, touching her now and then and leading her by the hand around the sitting room and kitchen, trying to make her feel involved in various activities.

At 11pm Rose bade Jill "sweet dreams", repeated her invitation to please make herself at home and, after a short taped update to her mother, went to bed. Lying awake for some time, it did occur to Rose that some people might find her actions a little strange. Here she was, calmly trying to sleep in a wind battered isolated house, with a reanimated dead person keeping watch in the room below. It made her think, with a thrill, of TV ghost stories. And that got her off to sleep.

Saturday, December 11th, 1965

Rose woke shortly after 7.30 in the morning. It was still rather dark outside but she put on her cotton robe and went downstairs to greet her guest and make breakfast.

Jill was sitting down in one of Rose's old armchairs. More than that, she'd managed to dress herself properly in the garment that had hung so ridiculously on her angular shape only the previous day. And her body had filled out, the flesh softening and losing a good deal of its mummified, leathery quality. The hole in the middle of her face had filled in and there was a small bump which signified the presence of an emerging nose. Rose hadn't been able to guess how old Jill might have been at the point of her death beforehand, but now she looked middle aged, similar in years to Rose herself. The eyes were fully open and the lips were gently parted.

Rose was astonished at the transformation. She knelt on the floor in front of Jill and took both her hands. They were warm – and she was breathing.

"Oh my! Look at you!" Rose could not contain a gasp of astonishment as Jill lifted her head and looked directly at her. But she wore an expression of such deep sadness that Rose could hardly contain her tears. She put her arms around Jill and hugged her. Jill didn't resist the gesture, though Rose's spontaneous warmth was not similarly returned. Rose drew back from the embrace, and carefully examined Jill's cheeks, shoulders, etc. Jill's body felt alive, though she remained visibly worn and lined. Her skin had lost its peaty darkness and had acquired a deep yellow hue.

"Can you speak?"

There was no answer, although Jill's eyes remained fixed on her.

"I'm going to make you a cup of tea," said Rose, and pushing herself up from the floor made her way to the kitchen. Moments later she was back with a tea cup which she set on a small table at Jill's right side before returning to the kitchen to make toast and jam. Breakfast was unsuccessful. Rose munched and drank but it was as if Jill did not even see the food. "Marmite?" asked Rose, hopefully, and brought some. There was not so much as a flicker from Jill, and her tea went cold.

There was the sound of an engine pulling to a halt in the road, followed by Tommy Widdop's footsteps along the front garden path. Rose opened the door before Tommy had dropped the letters through the flap.

"Morning Miss 'Eadlam."

"Hello Tommy. How are you?"

"Very nice of you to ask. I'm well, thank you."

"I have a question."

"Away you go…"

"Do you have any idea who lived in the house before we did?"

"Well Miss 'Eadlam, that's a long way back. Way before I was on this route. In fact I'd have just been a nipper. When did you move in?"

"It was 1923."

"1923… I would've been ten years old."

Rose sensed movement behind her. Jill had moved into the hallway and stood in the dimness, looking at the open door. Tommy peered past Rose, trying to make out the figure.

"Got company?" he said to Rose. Then, "'ow do!" to Jill. No response.

"My friend Jill," said Rose.

"Nice to meet you, Jill," called out Tommy, waving.

"Who would know, Tommy? Any ideas? Who could I ask?"

"Well, let's see... Who would have been around here that far back? Jimmy Jackson's dad of course. Other than that... Well, Doris Naseby lived up at High House for ages..."

"Yes, of course," said Rose. "I remember her. She came over and said hello just after we moved in. Her husband had died she said. Invited us up to the house. We never went..."

"High House is owned by a pair from London now," said Tommy. "It's mostly empty but they turn up now and then. Somerville's the name. They've owned the place for about twenty years, ever since Doris left."

"Can't think of anyone else then?"

"Well, nothing comes to mind. These houses – they're so out of the way, you see. A lot of people don't even know they're here. You'll probably 'ave to search the local records for title deeds or summat like that. I think old Bill 'Ardaker used to own this place – used to let it, but 'e's been dead for years now. There's a son somewhere but I couldn't tell you exactly where. 'Ardaker Farm changed hands long ago."

"Okay. Thanks Tommy."

"Sorry I can't be more 'elp Miss 'Eadlam."

"That's alright. Let me know if anything else comes to mind please."

"I certainly will."

Closing the door: "Have a good day then Tommy."

"Same to you Miss 'Eadlam." Just before the door closed completely he shouted out, "Tarra Jill!"

In the darkened hallway Rose turned to Jill and took her hands.

"I'm going to find out what happened to you. I think you've come back for a reason, and I'm going to help."

Jill's face remained impassive but Rose, with delight, felt her hands squeezed. She returned the gesture. "Oh my poor love. You leave it to me."

There was an old bicycle propped up in the outhouse. Agnes had used it regularly and Rose had kept it going although cycling was not an activity she enjoyed. Nevertheless, needs must. Jackson Farm was close to Stanghow, about eight miles away by road and it would probably be quickest to get there under her own steam. She pumped up the tyres, checked the wheels, listened to the noon weather forecast, got on and pedalled towards her destination.

The farmhouse was about half a mile off the road at the end of a dirt track. The fields on either side of the track were completely empty of livestock and Rose guessed they were inside for safety, especially after the recent terrible weather.
She arrived just after two o'clock and knocked at the door. After a few seconds it swung open and Rose found herself face to face with a large woman aged about sixty.
"Hello, what can I do you for?"
Rose had never met Jenny, Jimmy's wife. She said, "I'm looking for Jimmy. I'm one of his customers."
"Oh," said Jenny, "Nuthin' wrong I 'ope."
"No, no," Rose replied. "I just want to say hello and pick his brains about something."
The woman nodded her head and held out her hand. "I'm Jenny, Jimmy's wife. Nice to meet you."
"Rose Headlam. Likewise."
Jenny invited Rose into the house and called for Jimmy who was luckily at home for the day.
"Now then, now then Miss 'eadlam! We don't often see you away from Boulby Cliff. This is an unexpected pleasure. It must be somethin' important."
"I'll get 'kettle on," said Jenny, and left Rose and Jimmy together.
Rose began. "Well, I'm just curious. I'm doing a bit of research. Do you know who occupied the house before us? It would have been a very long time ago."
"Well, let me think… Aye. I used to go on 'rounds wi' me old dad

and we used to deliver to all 'ouses on that lane. I'd've been a little'un at 'time. There were a young couple in there before 'war. What were their name?... Oh dear, me memory's not what it were. Nice bloke, 'e was. And she, she were a pretty lass. Aye, I remember 'er. I used to look forward to them visits." He was shaking his head from side to side, picturing the woman in his mind. "They 'ad some trouble or summat. I can't bring to mind now what it were. Some other bloke turned up. Me old dad weren't impressed wi' 'im at all. 'E were a local troublemaker I seem to recall. Oh dear... I can't remember any o' 'details though. Ee, I 'aven't thought about them in years. She *were* a pretty lass…my, my, my…"

Jenny arrived with tea and biscuits.

Jimmy continued. "You've been livin' in that 'ouse for so many years, Miss 'eadlam. Why 'sudden interest? – if you don't me askin'."

"Oh, it's just something I dug up in the garden."

Jimmy threw up his hands and laughed. "Oh dear, oh dear! Not a body, I 'ope."

Rose laughed back, and Jimmy realised with a start that he'd never seen Rose do such a thing in all these years.

But then she stopped laughing, and he realised she hadn't answered him yes or no. He felt instantly alarmed, knit his brow and leant back in his chair in horror.

"Bloomin' 'eck! It *weren't* a body, werrit?"

"No," she lied. "I've got a bee in my bonnet about something. That's all."

Jimmy was relieved. The three of them chatted while the tea and biscuits were consumed. Then Rose got up to leave. "Thank you, Jimmy. And nice to meet you, Jenny."

Jimmy nodded. Jenny replied, "And very nice to meet *you*, Miss Headlam."

Rose surprised herself by spontaneously offering her first name. "Call me Rose – if you wouldn't mind."

"Rose," said Jimmy. Jenny smiled.

"I've been thinking recently… we go through our lives mostly ignoring what's around us. Sometimes we're given the chance to

do something for someone else… and that makes us alive!" Then she said, slowly, "*Brings us to life.*" She caught Jimmy's eyes with a penetrating vision: "Don't you think so? I think people should watch out for each other." She was smiling. She thought they were both probably a little puzzled, but they didn't offer any reply.
They saw Rose to the door and she hopped on her bike. She began to pedal away but Jimmy called out to her: "'Old up, Rose! I've just 'ad a thought. You could ask old Doris Naseby."
Rose stopped the bicycle. "Doris? She must be dead, surely?"
"No, I don't think so. I think she's in a nursin' 'ome in Whitby. That's the last I 'eard. I'm pretty sure she's still alive."

Rose pedalled back to Boulby Cliff and found Jill sitting forlornly in the kitchen, still wrapped in the dressing gown. She checked the time. It was a quarter to six and she needed to turn on the television.
"Jill, my love, I have to spend about half an hour upstairs. If you can manage the stairs come and find me. Otherwise I'll be back before you know it…" And she was gone.
A few minutes later Rose was sitting in front of *Counter Plot*, the fifth part of The Doctor's latest adventure with the Daleks. The overhead electric light was off and Rose was settled, completely absorbed.
She became aware of the stairs creaking, then the door opening. A moment later Jill was sitting next to her in Agnes's favourite armchair. Rose put out her hand and took Jill's. She glanced across at one point and couldn't tell in the gloom whether Jill's attention was on the screen or not. Probably not, she thought. Jill was here in the room because Rose was here.

Sunday December 12th, 1965

In the morning Rose found Jill in the television room, still sitting in Agnes's chair, still wrapped in the dressing gown. Some of the yellow glaze had gone and Rose began to revise her estimate of Jill's age. Yesterday she'd thought fifty or fifty-five. Now Jill looked perhaps ten years younger than that.

"Good morning, Jill. Breakfast time! Come on down, if you can. I'll put the kettle on."

Rose was soon busy with toast and tea in the usual way. After a few minutes she heard the stairs creaking as Jill made her way down. Rose walked into the hallway and watched her progress. Jill seemed more supple than yesterday, the movements of her limbs very much smoother. Was she really going to recover fully? Rose thought hard – *to recover fully from death?* She recalled the old tale of Kate and Amos. It was a horror story that hadn't ended well. And the legends told of something similar with Moll and her little sister Phyllis, although that story was apocryphal – Moll had always denied it and laughed with scorn whenever it was mentioned. But now? Rose was thinking – Have I done it? Just through instinct and love – *have I brought this person back from the dead?* A thrill ran through her.

Jill sat in the kitchen while Rose ate breakfast but again showed no interest in consuming anything. She remained silent and blank.

Rose had made up her mind to seek out Doris Naseby. If she really was still alive she must surely be a tremendous age and there was consequently no time to lose. She also had to follow up any possible lead that might be made with the old Hardaker farm, so gathering pen and paper, she wrote to the farm manager:

Boulby Cliff House
nr. Boulby
Cleveland

Sunday, December 12th, 1965

Dear Sir,

I am the owner and resident of Boulby Cliff House. My family moved here in 1923 and I am doing some research on previous occupants. I believe that Farmer William Hardaker used to own this property before WW1. I understand that Mr Hardaker died some time ago but wondered if you might have any information that might relate to my research. I am particularly interested in the period from about 1900 to

1923 but would be equally interested in earlier records if they exist. I hope you will not find my letter an intrusion.

Yours faithfully,

Rose Headlam (Miss)

She informed Jill of her intentions for the day, put on her hat and coat against the miserable weather and walked up to the main road to catch the bus to Boulby. Once there she posted her letter, found a telephone box and, with the aid of the directory and an operator, began to work through local nursing homes, beginning with those in Whitby. There were a lot of them and it took her forty minutes of loose change to track Doris down.

"Doris Naseby? Aye, Doris is 'ere."

Rose was thrilled. "She is? That's wonderful! Can I pay her a visit please?"

"Are you a relative?"

"No. But I was Doris's neighbour for many years. We didn't know each other very well and she may not remember me, but I'm doing some research on the area and I thought Doris might be able to help."

The voice at the other end: "Aye, I'm sure that'll be fine. Doris is frail though – she's ninety-nine and doesn't 'ear very well."

"I'm sure I'll manage. When would be a good time?"

"Why don't you come today, if you're about?"

"I am. I can be there in (she checked the address in the telephone book) about an hour and a half."

"They'll be 'avin' lunch then, and a lot of our folks like to nap after lunch. Would four o'clock do you?"

Rose agreed, congratulated herself, and took the bus to Whitby. In earlier years she would have used the train, but the railway line had closed in 1958. There was a flower stall in the main bus station and Rose bought Doris a colourful bouquet. Then she treated herself to a roast lunch in a hotel near the harbour. She accompanied her meal with a half pint of *Double Diamond*, recalling the old television advertisement, *The Beer the Men Drink*. Rose thought she could probably drink it too but it made her head swim and

she found that she couldn't walk afterwards without staggering a little. Fortunately she had some extra time, so was able to recover before taking a taxi to the Esk Valley Nursing Home in Stainsacre, two and a half miles from Whitby town centre. Worried that her breath might smell of beer, she found an old packet of mints in her handbag and sucked on one for a few minutes.
On the dot of four o'clock she was sitting next to Doris Naseby.

Doris's husband, Harold, had died suddenly of a heart attack in 1921. He'd been seven years older than Doris, who found herself alone at the age of fifty-five. She didn't remarry and there'd been no children so she led a solitary existence at High House. Although lonely she had local interests, went to church regularly, ran a book club in her own home, became a significant figure in a local horticultural society and tended her garden thoroughly. Her life was not unhappy. As time went on she became increasingly frail and found the stairs an ever greater problem. In 1946 she decided to move out of High House into a bungalow in Whitby, where she lived contentedly for some years. But her health continued to decline and In 1958, no longer able to cope by herself, she moved into the nursing home in which Rose found her.
"Hello Mrs Naseby."
"Call me Doris, dear."
"Thank you – Doris. I'm Rose, Rose Headlam. You probably don't remember me. I moved into Boulby Cliff House in 1923 with my mum, dad and gran. You came to say hello just after we arrived. Do you remember? They were Agnes and Edward – Ted. My gran was Mary but we always called her Moll. Do you remember? It was a long, long time ago."
"Moll… Rose…" Doris's eyes lit up. "Rosie Red! Yes, I remember you. You were a little girl – with lovely red hair. My goodness, is that you? You're all silver now…" She put out her hand and touched Rose's hair. "How old are you?"
"I'm fifty-one Doris."
"Fifty-one. I'm ninety-nine!"

"I know," smiled Rose. "You're doing well!"

A pause, then, "Ah, Boulby Cliff. I miss those days."

Rose took her hand. "Doris, can I ask you a few things please?"

"Go on then."

"Do you remember who lived in the house before we arrived?"

"Oh yes, I could never forget them. I remember them *very* well. George and Alice lived there. George and Alice… oh, I forget their last name – it was quite an unusual name – crunchy, sounded crunchy…"

"Tell me what you remember about them."

The act of remembering seemed to further invigorate Doris. She sat forward a little, her eyes gleaming.

"Well, they moved in straight after they got married. I know that because we went down to Boulby Cliff to say hello the day after they moved in. That was a few years before the war – I can't remember exactly when. They were a nice couple, young. They kept themselves to themselves though – we didn't see them very often. There was some trouble and George went off to war. Alice – she got together with a really nasty piece of work. It was the talk of the town for a while. This fellow though – used to work for me at High House when he was younger. Pinched things. I caught him one day – interfering with a girl in my greenhouse! Verrill, Stephen Verrill was his name. How Alice ever got involved with him I'll never understand. I heard George had left and I went down to the house one day to see if I could help – and there they were – Verrill and Alice sharing the house together. She didn't look happy at all. He shut the door in my face. Foul little rat he was! Then they left together and no one ever saw them again. Emigrated to Canada. That would have been about 1916."

She fell silent. Rose was thinking hard, trying to sift all the new information.

"Do you know where George and Alice were married, Doris?"

"*Where* they were married? No, I'm afraid I don't dear. It was probably local though – I think I remember them saying they'd come straight to the house from their reception."

Rose nodded. "Doris, you've been such a big help. Thank you so much."

"My pleasure dear," she smiled. "Rosie Red!"

Rose kissed her on the cheek and began to rise from her seat. "If you remember anything else please write and let me know."

"I will dear. Thanks for visiting me – I don't get many visitors. It was nice."

"Bless you, Doris. Take care."

Rose waved and began to get up but Doris suddenly said, "Cromack. That was their name. George and Alice Cromack."

On the way home Rose found herself thinking hard. It seemed unlikely that the information gleaned from Doris could help with the identification of Jill. All the people in her story seemed to have left the house and gone on with their lives in other places. Jill surely couldn't be Alice, because Alice had emigrated to Canada with Verrill. It was all still a puzzle. Perhaps Rose had been mistaken when she interpreted Jill's small physical gesture as an indication that she recognised Jimmy's name. Maybe Jill had been in the earth before the turn of the century, perhaps long before. Rose had no idea how old the bones had been.

She got off the bus shortly after half past seven that evening and walked the mile down the lane back to the house. She opened the front door, took off her hat and coat and walked into the sitting room. It was in darkness but she was aware of Jill standing in the gloom. Rose switched on the light and gasped in shock. This was not the Jill she had left in the house this morning. Of that figure, only the dressing gown remained. Rose saw a slender, attractive young woman, probably in her late twenties, with fine shoulder length brown hair, bright blue eyes and healthy, glowing skin.

"Oh my goodness!" exclaimed Rose, staggering forward with her hand clasped to her mouth. Jill reached out and caught her, although her blank expression remained and she uttered no sound. Gathering herself, though still rather breathless, Rose said, "Oh… oh, my! Look at you! I can hardly believe it! My, but you're *beautiful*, my love!"

Later, when Rose was calmer, they sat together in the kitchen.

Rose explained to Jill that she was trying very hard to piece together various bits of evidence that might eventually reveal the truth of who she was and what had become of her.
"Why can't you speak, Jill? Why can't you tell me? There's something missing." Then, excitedly, "Can you write?" Rose produced a paper and pencil but Jill took no notice of it.
While Jill sat patiently, like a statue, Rose thought hard. Jill had come back into being at least partly because of Rose's own actions – that she believed. But she also sensed that her part in Jill's story would extend beyond the mere discovery of her true identity.

Rose prepared to go to bed at half past ten. She led Jill to the second bedroom and sorted out a few items of clothing for her. Jill sat quietly on the bed, hunched forward, hands on knees. Rose wished her good night, closed the door and, tape running, brought her mother up to date with developments.
During the dark of the night Rose lay awake, pondering what the next move might be. She did not believe that Jill was Alice Cromack but she needed to find a photograph of Alice to set her mind at ease. How to achieve that? According to Doris the Cromacks had moved into Boulby Cliff House on the night of their wedding. So the first action might be to track down a record, a document relating to the marriage. Rose did not know quite how to go about this. Where would such a thing be kept? She worried about it for an hour or two before sleep took her.

Monday December 13th, 1965

The next morning Rose woke with a headache. Nevertheless, she'd summoned sufficient energy by nine o'clock to cycle to Boulby and once more plant herself in the telephone booth that had proved so advantageous in tracking down Doris Naseby. She'd worked out a method that might help her hunt for documentation about George and Alice's marriage. It involved contacting lots of churches. Rose had heard the phrase "parish records" and thought it likely that wedding documents and other pertinent papers might be preserved in them.

If George and Alice had been married nearby it seemed reasonable to begin her search by assuming that their wedding had taken place within, say, ten miles of the house. So she telephoned the vicar of Roxby church. He was very helpful and spoke kindly, explaining that the records were passed to the county council, although it was common for individual churches to retain a copy of the documentation relating to many events. Rose explained that she was looking for information about a wedding that would have taken place between 1905 and 1914. The names of the people involved were George and Alice Cromack. If it wasn't too much to ask, would he mind having a look please? That would be fine. Could he telephone her later? Rose explained that she had no telephone but could pass by Roxby church on her bicycle in the afternoon. It was so arranged.

Next she phoned the vicar of St Hilda's Church, Hinderwell, repeating her story. The vicar explained that he did not have the time to personally execute such a search but that Rose would be welcome to check the records herself if she wished. She received a similar response from the incumbents of various churches in Staithes, Easington and Port Mulgrave. She thought it might take two or three full days to hunt through the files of all those churches. If her search was unsuccessful she would make another selection of possible venues and carry on.

So, she was going to church, a rare event for her. The old family had always shunned Christian buildings – except for funerals. Even then it was only seen as a convenient way of dealing with death – allowing the system to take care of it. But in more recent generations the attitude had softened a little. Rose's father Edward had insisted that he and Agnes must be married in a church. It was the first such wedding ceremony in the history of the family. Moll, though clearly unimpressed, had not blocked Edward's wishes and had attended the wedding without too many complaints, although she had frightened the vicar a little with her rather glum and forbidding countenance. Edward also insisted that Rose must be baptised. Again, just a dismissive sniff from Moll (what did such nonsense mean anyway? Ridiculous rituals didn't change anything...). So Rose was baptised, together with her mother Agnes, at Glaisdale church on the morning of Sunday August 9th, 1914, five days into the war.

Rose had no idea what shade of Christian (if any) George and Alice felt themselves to be, which complicated the search for the marriage record. Protestant, Roman Catholic, Methodist...? She had to be thorough and inclusive.

She began with a search through the records of Our Lady Star of the Sea in Staithes, simply because she liked the name. A lot of marriages had taken place there in the first two decades of the twentieth century, but George and Alice were not listed among them. She worked through most of the other churches in the town omitting only those to which she had not been able to gain access. That took most of the day, leaving only time enough to cycle to Hinderwell, where she spent an hour checking through the records before pedalling on to Roxby. The vicar shook her hand, told her how nice it was to meet her and informed her that his thorough search of the parish documents had uncovered no Cromack wedding during the period in which Rose was searching, or at any time as far as he could see.

It had been a tiring and disappointing day. Dusk had arrived and Rose faced a cold journey back to Boulby Cliff. Easington was close as the crow flew, but the route over the hill from Roxby was arduous and roundabout. Rose decided to put it off until the morning.

She found Jill sitting quiet and inactive at home. Rose knew in her heart that Jill was waiting for something but could not yet fathom exactly what it was.

Tuesday December 14th, 1965

It was a strange sort of morning, the drizzle falling in soft curtains while the sun tried to cut through the murk. Rose, increasingly fit, cycled to Easington where she met the vicar of All Saints Church.

He made her welcome, setting her up with a chair, a table and a pot of tea in the vestry. He'd already taken out the various books of records and had arranged them for her in order of date, starting with 1905. Assuring Rose that she would find him in the vicarage he left her to her own devices and she began work.

She worked carefully through the immaculately kept documents event by event. 1905, 06, 07, 08, 09, 1910. July 23rd. George Cromack and Alice Eves.

Her heart almost stopped. She'd found them. Rose made a note of the date and time of the wedding, thanked the vicar heartily (he was very pleased to have been able to help – she was welcome to the church at any time. Sunday worship took place at 10am and 6pm and the church was home to a thriving branch of the Mothers' Union…).

On her bike and away, Rose's mind raced. She had a date, she had a venue. It seemed likely that there could have been photographs. If they'd been professionally taken they might still survive somewhere.

Back at the Boulby telephone kiosk she hunted through the listings for photographers, hoping she might find one with roots that went back more than fifty years. She spent the remainder of the morning on the telephone either to photographers themselves or attempting to get ideas from the longsuffering operator, but with no luck. She could find no photographic firm with roots stretching further back than twenty years or so. Rose was stumped. She sat in a nearby café over a cup of tea and pondered.

Twenty minutes later she was on the telephone to Whitby library asking after photographic archives. The woman at the library suggested Whitby museum, so Rose called the institution right away. A man answered and introduced himself as the curator. Yes, the museum had a growing collection of historic photographs, largely of old Whitby street scenes, etc. dating back to the middle of the nineteenth century. It was, however, very unlikely that Rose would find a specific wedding photograph. Perhaps she would have more luck contacting private collectors who might have personal archives of old photographs. He suggested that she write to the Whitby Camera Club with specific details of what she was looking for, and provided her with the secretary's name, address and telephone number.

At four o'clock Rose found herself in the living room of a small house near the harbour, taking tea with David Ingram, secretary of the club.

"A wedding in Easington in July 1910. It's not outside the realms of possibility that someone *may* have what you're looking for. We're fortunate to live in such a pretty town with such an interesting history. Whitby has always attracted keen photographers. A handful of our members have gathered together large collections of photographs from the past. I believe two or three of them have made a hobby of buying up old archives."

"Well, that sounds promising," said Rose.

"Let's make a few calls and see what we can do," said Ingram, picking up the receiver and popping open a small spring directory.

The first call went unanswered but the second, to a Mr Simon Ellerby, received an enthusiastic response. Delighted to have the opportunity to entertain an interested party he invited Rose to come straight round and make herself at home.

Shortly before five o'clock Rose was in Mr Ellerby's huge house on Cleveland Way, which overlooked the beach and the North Sea. He was eccentric, noisy, blustering and enthusiastic. So was his wife. His house consisted of room after room of cases and stands of archived photographs arranged by creator and date. He manifested his delight at Rose's interest by fussing noisily around her as much as he could while she searched through his vast collection, section by section.

In the fulness of time Rose came to the table marked *Filing's Photography, Whitby, 1901-1940*. The photographs were meticulously organised. Ellerby informed her that he'd purchased Filing's entire archive when the firm went into liquidation during the war. Arthur Filing and his son Peter, had been keen archivists and had thoroughly documented all their work over nearly forty years.

From that point it was easy. Rose found the year 1910, then July

23rd, Easington. There was only one envelope of prints. Rose opened the packet and took them out. Simon was suddenly quiet, observing Rose's response. She was silent, but the tears gathered on her chin. Simon raised his eyebrows in mute surprise.
There was George. And there was Jill. Alice. Jill was Alice Cromack.

Rose asked to borrow the pictures, promising to return them safely. Simon Ellerby agreed, and was delighted to have been able to help.
Rose took the bus back to Boulby, picked up her bicycle and pedalled home in excitement, arriving at 9.30pm. She found Jill sitting silently in the dark, leaning forward in her accustomed posture, hands on knees. Rose switched on the light and discovered that Jill had dressed herself in a pale blue floral frock. It was cold in the house but she exhibited no sign of discomfort. Rose settled herself in the chair opposite and composed herself, looking hard at her companion. Then, very quietly, she said…
"Alice."
Alice looked up quickly and for the first time Rose saw a look of surprise on her face. Rose was holding up one of Alice's wedding photographs so she could see it. Alice's breath left her body. She rushed forward on her knees and took the picture in her hands, bursting into floods of noisy tears as she did so. They were the first vocalised sounds Rose had heard from her and, lips puckering, she began to cry in sympathy.
Alice looked at her with an expression that asked, "How?"
Rose, trying hard to gain control of her own sobbing, described how she'd tracked the photos down. Then she said, "Alice. I think there was some trouble between you and George. I don't know what it was, but George went away. Then, somehow you became involved with someone called Stephen Verrill. I think he killed you. He buried you in the garden and ran away. All the time we lived here – all these years – we never knew you were there – in the garden. No one ever knew – until now."

Wednesday December 15th, 1965

Rose had never felt so energised. There was no stopping her. She lay awake in the night, formulating her next move. She had to find out what had happened to George and to Stephen Verrill. Her instinct told her that George had most likely died in the war, but in any case she'd probably be able to find his military records. She might also be able to dig up some evidence of Stephen's emigration to Canada.

At breakfast, while Alice sat silently opposite her, gazing at her wedding photographs, Rose wrote a letter to "The Ministry of Defence". She had no idea as to whom she should be addressing the letter, or even to which department, trusting simply that it would eventually wing its way to some appropriate desk:

Boulby Cliff House
nr. Boulby
Cleveland

Wednesday, December 15th, 1965

Dear Sir,

I wonder if I may ask your assistance. I am trying to trace a record for Mr George Cromack. Mr Cromack lived in the house now occupied by myself in the years immediately preceding World War 1. I have learned that he signed up for the military early in the conflict and have no record of him beyond that. At the time he enlisted I think he would have been in his late twenties or early thirties. I imagine he probably did not survive the war, but you may have some record of what became of him. Any information would be much appreciated.

I hope to hear from you soon.

Yours faithfully,

Rose Headlam (Miss)

Rose needed the telephone again so she pedalled to her familiar spot in Boulby. She called Whitby Library and asked how she might find a particular emigration record from 1915 or '16. The librarian suggested that she search through microfilm data. Rose felt a little intimidated by that and asked how it might be done. Her grasp of modern technology extended to switching on the television and the tape recorder. She knew roughly what the term "microfilm" meant as she'd heard it mentioned in spy movies, but considered it unlikely that she would be able to successfully grapple with such a futuristic thing. The librarian suggested that Rose might employ a researcher to undertake the task on her behalf. That sounded much more reassuring and Rose breathed a sigh of relief.

"What's the name of the person you're searching for?" asked the librarian.

"It's Stephen Verrill."

"And what's your interest in him?"

"I believe he lived in my house for a while, a long time ago, back at the start of World War 1. He's believed to have emigrated to Canada so there could be some record of departure or arrival for him."

"I see," replied the librarian. "We'll need to take payment for this in advance so perhaps you'd like to look in at the library at some point?"

"Yes," said Rose. "I'll come right away."

She chained up her bicycle and within minutes was on the bus to Whitby.

Rose paid the researcher's fee at Whitby library, although she was told the work would actually be carried out in York. The researcher would look for the name Stephen Verrill in relation to emigration documents, passenger lists, general public records and newspapers. Rose, having been awakened so recently to this science fiction-like method of research, wondered if perhaps she should look for George in the same way. After a little thought she decided against it, for now. She'd wait and see what the search for Stephen turned up first. Maybe the MOD might come up with something on George in the meantime.

25. BILL AND STEPHEN

Monday February 12th, 1934, Gorbals, Glasgow

Bill Greenwood lay on the floor of the gents in The Anchorage bar on Eglinton Street. A few of his teeth lay around him in shallow puddles of his blood. His hands were tied. Stephen Verrill squatted before him.
"You always thought you knew best, Bill. Always steppin' in where you weren't wanted. Always tryin' to take control of things you 'ad no business in."
Bill sputtered through bloodied lips, "You were a worthless gobshite in the old days, Stephen, and you're nothing but a sick piece of shite now."
Stephen rose and booted Bill in the face. Kneeling again he produced a small knife and held it close to Bill's swollen eyes. "I'm not in a hurry. I could slice off a few of your fingers. It might take a while with this little blade, but I'd enjoy the noises you'd make. Or I could slice your eyelids off…"

Bill Greenwood had led a varied life since the war. He'd come back from Flanders and taken a job as a gravedigger in a York cemetery, then as a barman in a pub in the city. He'd soon worked himself up in the trade and found himself running his own bar. As his mother grew older and more frail Bill felt compelled to be closer to her, and so in 1928 he'd returned to Kilmarnock, the town of his birth, taking over the management of a bar on West Langlands Street. In 1930, shortly after the death of his mother, Bill had been invited to take over The Anchorage on Eglinton Street, south of the Clyde in the historic Gorbals district of Glasgow.
Glasgow was home to a flourishing culture of rival gangs, particularly on the east and south sides. The city had seen mass immigration in the preceding decades and unemployment was at a very high level. Protection and extortion rackets were rife and clashes

between gangs were common. The local community respected Bill. He was a Scot by birth and was known as a reliable and trustworthy man. He had acquaintances in rival factions and tried not to take sides.

But he worked in a bar and inevitably overheard things. The police would occasionally quiz him for information, for advance mutterings of riots, muggings, burglaries and other crimes. Sometimes Bill had the information they wanted, sometimes he guessed it, always trying to weigh up the value and likely outcome of what he gave away. He hoped that he might, in a small way, contribute to minimising any misfortune or violence. After all, many of the men involved had wives and families and Bill always thought of the impact on them. Bill's own relationships with women had always ended badly so he remained alone as far as possible.

Then one day in 1933 Stephen Verrill turned up at the Anchorage. He sat there over a pint of heavy and looked steadily at Bill, an ugly smile on his face. It had been eighteen years since Bill had last seen Stephen, and though the face was very familiar Bill could not at first place him.

After a while Stephen said, shaking his head, "You're jokin', right?"

"Do I know you?"

"Ha! You don't remember…"

Recognition came to Bill, revulsion following quickly. "Stephen Verrill."

A chuckle. "You got there."

"What do you want here?"

"Nothin' Bill. I live 'ere."

"Since when?"

"A while."

Bill shook his head and walked away, instructing one of the other bar staff to serve Stephen if necessary. Bill didn't want to look at him.

From that moment the Anchorage became one of Stephen's regular haunts. He knew that his presence in the pub intimidated Bill and found it entertaining to make the older man uncomfortable.

Stephen had been living in Glasgow for some time. He'd fled the scene of a crime in England in 1930, had come to Scotland and taken rooms in a tenement above a popular bar on Byres Road. He quickly found a way into the local criminal underworld, and before long he made a name for himself in the gang culture. In 1933 he moved to the south side to be closer to his friends in one particular Catholic mob.

Bill had no qualms about marking Stephen out to the police as a likely source of trouble.

Stephen was eagle-eyed. He knew that Bill had an association with the law and watched for an opportunity to catch him out.

Malicious static permeated the pub during late January and early February. Trouble brewed along with the beer, and local goons rekindled vendettas based on long-held hatreds. The gangs had begun to squabble about rival businesses and a riot became likely. Bill picked up garbled details of dates and times, and when the opportunity arose he passed them to the police. The day of the clash came, the constabulary stepped in and arrests were made. There had been a tip-off. Who was responsible? Stephen Verrill volunteered an answer.

On the evening of February 12th Stephen and two pals arrived at the Anchorage and ordered drinks. They were still there at the close of business and Bill sensed danger. By eleven thirty the bar was almost empty. Stephen's two thugs intimidated the remaining bar staff out of the building while Stephen himself sat watching Bill. The doors were locked and the fun began.

Stephen had ordered his men to tie Bill's hands and soften him up with their fists. Then he told them to make themselves at home behind the bar and leave the remainder of the job to him. Once the two of them were alone he'd given Bill the same kind of thrashing that Stephen received from him that night at Boulby Cliff all those long years ago. Revenge was sweet.

Stephen had offered to remove Bill's eyelids...

"Get it over with," spat Bill. "Just kill me and be on your way."

"I ain't ready for that yet," Stephen spoke quietly, regaining his breath after his prolonged pounding of Bill. "You remember that night? That night *I* was on the end of *your* boot? You – you thought you were the knight in shining armour. You remember what you said?"

"I do. I'd kill you. There's no reason that scum like you should continue to breathe."

"Hm," Stephen replied. "When you were gone – that night – when you were gone I took Alice into the garden and stuck a pitchfork through 'er. Then I smashed her pretty head in with a hammer."

Bill stared at him in disbelief.

"Yep," said Stephen. "I buried her in the strawberries. No one ever found out. You didn't save her, Bill."

Bill did not reply.

The sound of some kind of commotion in the bar carried into the toilets. There were two gunshots. Stephen rose and fumbled as he tried to unholster his weapon. The door flew open and a single figure appeared – a young man dressed in a long black coat and wide-brimmed hat. Bill vaguely recognised him. The man carried a gun, and with no hesitation at all he aimed it at Stephen and fired. Stephen's right knee burst open in a little shower of blood and bits of bone. A few wisps of smoke quickly dispersed around the hole in his trouser leg. He dropped his own weapon and collapsed with a scream of pain, clutching the wound. Blood flowed through his interlaced fingers. Pleading, he began shuffling backwards towards the wall. The man followed and fired a second shot into Stephen's left thigh. Two more shots followed, disabling both his arms.

Seconds later Bill's rescuer cut the cords binding his hands. The man, whom Bill was still trying to identify, handed him a razor, said "He's yours," and then turned and left, the door crashing behind him.

Bill was dazed by the speed of events, but after a moment stood painfully and opened the blade. Stephen was weeping, pleading. "No. Please...", his panic rising in a crescendo as his executioner approached.

Bill knelt behind Stephen and raised him to a sitting position, then used his left arm to force Stephen's head backwards, exposing his neck. He thought of Alice, helpless and terrified in the bath that night. Bill said, "This is for that poor girl. Go to Hell, you bastard," and slit Stephen's throat.

26

Thursday December 16th – Monday December 20th, 1965

There seemed to be nothing more that Rose could do so she sat at home with Alice, hoping that further information would arrive in the mail. Alice didn't move very much, although she would occasionally sit next to Rose in front of the television. Rose busied herself in the kitchen, often with the radio on. She would chat to Alice, but of course received no response other than through Alice's eyes. At night Alice would withdraw to the second bedroom but Rose never found the bed slept in or disturbed in any way.

On the nineteenth, the Sunday before Christmas, Rose awoke, made her way down to the kitchen and found the back door ajar. She stepped outside, put her hand to her forehead to shield her eyes from the steep morning sun and looked down the garden path. The potting shed door was open and she could see Alice sitting inside in her usual posture, hunched forward, hands on knees, head down. She was still dressed in the blue floral frock that Rose had provided. As far as Rose could tell, she'd never taken it off or changed it. The air outside felt cold, and Alice wasn't wearing a coat. Rose quickly found an old one of her own, dressed herself warmly and made her way to the shed where she hung the garment around Alice's shoulders. Pulling up the second stool she cuddled up next to Alice, put her arms around her, and touched her forehead to Alice's hair.

"We'll get there, my dear. We will. Give it time and we shall sort it out. There's a circle to close, a circle to close – I know there is, and it will soon come clear." Drawing back a little she gave Alice a peck on the head. Her hair smelt clean and alive. Alice turned towards her, looked into Rose's eyes and kissed her on the forehead.

On Monday Jimmy Jackson arrived with the second half of Rose's

Christmas supplies. Inside the box was a selection of perishable goods. It had occurred to Rose that she should have cancelled this delivery. Agnes had always prepared their Christmas meals in the past, even last year, though she died on Boxing Day. Rose didn't have her mother's skill in the kitchen and she found the prospect of preparing an entire bird just for herself rather daunting – and she was quite sure that Alice would just sit and look at it. Nevertheless, here it all was.

"Ey up, Rose."

"Hello Jimmy. How's Jenny? Well I hope."

"Aye, she's just fine," he said, bustling past her to the kitchen where he deposited the box on the table. Alice was sitting in the front room at the time and Rose briefly wondered what the result might have been if Jimmy had bumped into her. She found the thought both amusing and disturbing.

Jimmy took Rose's hand and said, "You 'ave a reet nice Christmas, Rose. If you feel lonely we're just up 'road – I could come and pick you up. We'd be reet chuffed t'ave yer at 'farm."

"That's a very kind thought Jimmy. I'm used to being by myself though. It doesn't worry me. I've got the TV and the radio. I'm not short of things to do."

"Well, as I say – Merry Christmas, Rose, and a Happy New Year to yer!"

"And you too Jimmy. Give my best to Jenny."

Jimmy turned and retraced his steps along the front path to his van. As he turned to shut the gate his eyes caught sight of a figure at the sitting room window – a woman. Expressionless, she seemed to be looking directly at him. A chill much deeper than the cold of the day froze him to the spot. He peered hard in disbelief and the image of Alice came flooding to him across a gulf of fifty years. He concentrated his gaze, squinting, and supporting himself on the gate. It couldn't be… He blinked vigorously, shook his head, then looked again. The figure had disappeared. His heart was racing. He stood motionless for a while, then forced himself to take several deep breaths. He got back into the van but it was several minutes before he'd recovered enough to drive away safely.

Wednesday December 22nd, 1965

Tommy Widdop felt even more cheerful than usual and was looking forward to various Christmas parties and pub knees-ups. His boyhood love of Christmas had developed into an adult enthusiasm for festive social gatherings and his ebullience leaked from him as he went about his rounds. Rose heard his van draw up, followed by the sound of him singing *White Christmas* as he danced gracefully up the path. He was gone before she could open the door but there was a brown envelope with a York postmark on the mat. Rose opened it and began to read.

The microfilm search had revealed a number of different Stephen Verrills but only one fit the

parameters of date and locale. There was no emigration record relating to this particular Stephen Verrill as far as the researcher could tell. Neither did his name appear on any transatlantic passenger crossing. In fact the analyst had discovered very little about him other than his certificates of birth and death and details of his parents and brother. There was one piece of startling information though: a newspaper article relating the story of his probable murder in Glasgow in February 1934. The envelope contained a copy of the relevant passage, which had been taken from the now-defunct *Glasgow Clarion*, published on Thursday February 15th, 1934:

TRIPLE MURDER IN SOUTH SIDE TAVERN

The bodies of three men were discovered on Tuesday morning in The Anchorage public house on Eglinton Street. Two men in their twenties were found in the bar area. Both had been shot at close range and have yet to be identified. The body of a third man, identified as Mr Stephen Verrill, 37, of no fixed abode, was found in the gentlemen's lavatories. Mr Verrill had been shot four times at close range, although death was administered by a deep slash wound to the throat. Mr William Greenwood, landlord of the Anchorage, is missing. Police are appealing for information.

Stephen Verrill's mother, Margaret Black, was listed as one of those who'd perished in London during the Blitz of September 15th, 1940 aged 85. His father Clifford Verrill had been found dead on October 21st, 1915 aged 47. He'd apparently committed suicide. Stephen's brother Robert had passed away very recently, on September 28th, 1965 aged 73.

It seemed that Rose had missed the final connection to Stephen by only three months.
She read the information aloud to Alice who appeared unmoved by it.

Friday December 24th, 1965

Christmas Eve arrived and with it a big surprise. Tommy delivered a package sent from Harrogate. It contained a large handful of unopened letters tied together with string, as well as a note addressed to Rose:

Darley House, Harrogate
Tuesday, December 21

Dear Miss Headlam,

Your letter was forwarded to me by Philip Williamson, who bought Hardaker Farm when my father died in 1935. I was born only a few years before the first war and have no knowledge of the occupants of the house on Boulby Cliff at that time. I do have some recollection of you moving in though. In 1923 I would have been eleven years old. I remember my father expressing surprise that anyone would be interested in buying that property, it was so cut off. I don't recall anything much about the house I'm afraid, but I do remember my father was very taken with a little red haired lass. That must have been you!

I'm afraid I can't be very much help, although I can pass on these letters to you. They're all addressed to Mrs Alice Cromack at the house on Boulby Cliff. I don't know why my father kept them. They've been sitting in one of the draws of his old desk for donkey's years. Maybe you'll know what to do with them.

Good luck to you!
Peter Hardaker

Rose dropped the note and put her nose to the stack of old envelopes. They smelled musty, exposed to the light of day for the first time in decades. The uppermost envelope, clearly addressed to Alice, carried a postmark that read *Field Post Office*, and was stamped with the date February 8th, 1916. She thumbed through the stack. There were twenty-six letters.

The day was unusually bright and Rose found Alice sitting in the potting shed again, head down in her usual posture.
"Alice," she said, holding out the tied-up pile of envelopes. Alice reached out, took the letters and looked at the handwriting on the first envelope. Her shoulders became tense as she began to work at the string with her delicate fingers, and she was sniffing with tears before the knot was undone. Rose reached out a hand, and resting it on Alice's shoulder said "I'll leave you for a while, my love." She turned, retraced her steps to the kitchen, made herself a cup of tea and sat quietly, waiting.
The radio was on and she listened to a short interview with David Willcocks, director of the chapel choir at King's College. The choir was preparing for the broadcast of their carol service later in the afternoon. The lives of the boy choristers sounded very demanding, with several hours' rehearsal each day in addition to their school work. Every year since 1932 Rose, Agnes and Edward had huddled near the radio and listened to the annual broadcast of the service. It had become a ritual.
An hour passed. Rose looked out of the back door and caught sight of Alice. She was standing at the end of the garden, close to where the wall had collapsed, motionless, although her coat flapped a little in the breeze and her hair caught in the wind. She stood silently, gazing out to sea, the sheer drop to the ocean just a few yards in front of her. Rose walked to the potting shed and found the letters scattered about on the table top, all opened. She scanned them. They were all from George of course. News from

the front, pleas for forgiveness, how much he missed her, memories of their time together, promises of his unending love for her… Rose stepped out of the shed, slowly made her way along the path, and was soon standing next to Alice above the crash of the waves far below. Alice was staring into infinite distance. Her face shone and Rose could see that she'd been crying for a long time. Rose reached out and took her hand.

At three o'clock Rose and Alice sat close to the radio and listened to the service from King's. It was a strange experience for Rose. The previous year she'd listened to the service with her mother, just two days before Agnes disappeared into death. Now, one year on, she was sharing the broadcast with someone who had returned from that darkest of places. As the choir sang Elizabeth Poston's carol, *Jesus Christ the Apple Tree*, Rose visualised a seed hidden in the dark ground and pondered within herself the nature of rebirth, of redemption, forgiveness, hope, and the gentle, overwhelming certainty of love.

Saturday December 25th – Wednesday December 29th, 1965

Christmas itself was uneventful. Alice sat in the house, unmoving, and Rose felt too subdued and self-conscious to make a big fussy dinner for herself so the cooking was modest. In the early evening Rose and Alice sat together in front of the television. The episode of Doctor Who broadcast that day, *The Feast of Stephen*, was a curious comedic affair involving many sets and much chasing around through time and space. At the end of the episode the Doctor looked out of the television and wished the viewers, "…a happy Christmas to all of you at home!"
Rose was startled. "Well I never," she said. "What a thing!"
The night was quiet. Alice spent much of Boxing Day in the shed with George's letters. Tuesday was miserable, grey and raining – Wednesday the same. There seemed to be no resolution to the situation with Alice. Rose sat with her from time to time and read from *The Portrait of a Lady*. Alice remained silent and Rose didn't know what to do next, feeling rather frustrated and inadequate.

It was as if the world had paused.

But things changed the next morning. Tommy brought an envelope from London. Opening it, Rose found a letter from a Major Richard Tomlinson informing her that a search had been made for records relating to George Cromack. His team had found a number of individuals with that name, but only one seemed to fit Rose's description. They'd sent a communication to Sergeant George Cromack informing him of Rose's request for information. Sergeant Cromack would no doubt be in touch directly if he felt able to assist. Major Tomlinson hoped he'd been of some service and wished Rose well.

Rose took the letter to Alice, held it up and said, "Alice. George is alive."

Thursday December 30th, 1965

The next morning brought a letter from George.

Truro, December 22nd

Dear Miss Headlam,

Your letter to the MOD has been forwarded to me. I have to say, it was very strange to read this. My memories of life at Boulby Cliff House are both my happiest and my worst. So much time has elapsed since I lived there that your note seemed to be calling me from the past – I was last there 46 years ago. As you can see, the war didn't close my book and I'm still pottering about at the age of 80. I'm curious to know about your interest in me.

I look forward to your further communication.

Yours sincerely,

George Cromack

Rose took the letter to Alice and handed it over, saying nothing as she did so. It brought about an instant change. Alice rose from her seat in tears. But they were tears of joy – and she was smiling.

George had provided an address and telephone number. Rose lost no time – she got on her bicycle and pedalled to Boulby. Twenty minutes later she was speaking to George Cromack on the phone.

"Hello?"

"George? Is that George Cromack?"

"Yes, it is."

"I can't believe I'm actually talking to you!"

"I'm sorry – who is this?"

Rose was overexcited. She pulled herself together. "Oh – sorry. It's Rose Headlam, from Boulby Cliff."

"Ah. Miss Headlam, yes. What can I do for you?"

"Call me Rose – please. George. You need to come to Boulby. I can't tell you why, but you need to come here as soon as you can." There was a focused urgency in her tone and she hoped he was picking it up.

A pause. Then: "It's an awfully long way from here. To be honest, I don't want to open up memories by seeing the place again. Can't we do this on the phone?"

"Listen to me George. Please. I'm not a crackpot. But I'm giving you the most important message you'll ever hear in your life. You need to come here. Please trust me."

Silence. "What on earth is it?"

"I can't tell you on the phone."

Silence again. "All right. I'll pack a bag and book the journey. Can I stay? Have you got a spare room?"

"Yes George."

"I'll call you with the travel details."

"There's no phone at the house. I'll call you back on this number at one this afternoon. Will that be okay?"

"That'll be fine Rose. My goodness – what a mystery!"

27. GEORGE

1919-1957

For many years George lived in Bideford with his father David, always hoping for some communication from Alice. He spent his life in archaeology. Picking up the reins where he'd left them before the war, he led a successful career working for various universities and other bodies, becoming well respected in the field. He could never bring himself to divorce Alice, and despite her absence from his life he remained technically married to her. Despite occasional brief flirtations he was never able to form another lasting relationship and could never banish Alice from his thoughts. He made occasional attempts to trace Jane Grainger, but he never succeeded and spent all his life not knowing for sure whether he'd become a parent or not.

In the 1930s George suspended his professional work in order to care at home for his father who'd become very frail and who eventually passed away just before his ninety-eighth birthday, in 1938. When war broke out in September 1939 George was fifty-four years old, and being past the age of military conscription he enlisted in the Bideford Home Guard.

In the summer of 1945, a few months after VE Day, George spent a couple of days in Standon, hoping to find some trace of Alice. The drive from Bideford was the longest he'd ever made – a distance of some 240 miles – and he found it quite tiring. His heart was in his mouth as he turned off the main road and into the little town. There was the church, and the Star Inn. The village, with its very wide High Street, looked much as he remembered. He checked into the pub and dropped off his bag before wandering back and forth along the road – as far as the old workhouse almshouses to the south, then west past the Pudding Stone and down Paper Mill Lane to the ford. Finally he retraced his steps past the Star and along to the bakery. It was still there but had changed hands and no longer carried Benjamin's name. He crossed the street and walked back to the church. The sharp click of the latch, echoing in the lofty interior, summoned up vivid memories: the bustle of people at Benjamin's funeral, the scent of the flowers, the sea of black mourning clothes, Alice on his arm...

There was the curious slope of the nave – he'd forgotten about this odd feature of the church but his renewed acquaintance with it further sharpened the clarity of his recollection. It would have been possible, If one had left the big west door open, to set a marble rolling at the high altar and watch as it made its way down the chancel steps, along the nave and out onto the path. It could have rolled right through the front door of the Star had the road not been there to catch it.

It was cool in the old building, birdsong and the lowing of distant cattle gently piercing the stillness. There was the pew he'd shared with Alice at her father's funeral. The tombs and monuments, the ornate altar, the ancient stone coffin that had been discovered in the old east wall, the font, the organ – all as he remembered them. The chancel was dark, the nave bathed in light from the big west window. Emerging into the sunshine he took the path around the side of the building and up into the elevated churchyard behind. Benjamin's grave was still there of course, although it looked sunken and forgotten. George sat for a while on a bench and let his memories run in the sunshine.

He asked a few seasoned-looking people in the pub and in the local shops if they remembered Alice and Benjamin but got no luck. The church proved more fruitful. On the Sunday of his departure, summoned by the peal of bells from the famous 15th century detached tower, he attended the morning service, wondering if the older folk there might remember her. And they did – some with great affection, and by name. Always singing she was, always happy, her father's pride and joy. When George introduced himself as her husband some of them said they remembered him (George thought they probably didn't and were just being polite). But Alice and Benjamin were still fondly recalled, and that filled him with a warm glow. They excitedly asked if Alice had accompanied him to the village. It saddened him to tell them that they'd parted many, many years ago.

His little holiday had warmed his soul but had not lessened the ache in his heart. He didn't visit Standon again.

The six years of worldwide conflict began to melt into the past and George tried to interest himself once more in his profession, although he often felt tired and his heart wasn't in it. He dabbled for a few years before deciding to retire and move on. The landscape and history of Cornwall had become one of his primary interests in recent years so he decided that he'd put down his final roots, ending his days there. He sold the house in which he'd grown up and bought a property in Truro.

In retirement George kept abreast of discoveries and developments in archaeology, accepted a few honorary awards and appeared as guest speaker at occasional conferences. He attempted, without success, to learn the piano. Recalling Alice's prowess in her garden, he took an interest in horticulture although he had little talent for it. In 1956 he hired a gardener and took delight in the way the grounds around his house flourished and burst into colour. It often made him very emotional, sitting there alone, as memories of his lost love played over and over in his mind. Now and then he would say her name, breathing her wraith into the room with his lips.

"Alice…"

Out of curiosity George wrote to Kew and asked for information, including a list of gardeners. He found Dr Jeremy Silver listed on the staff. For months George held off writing to Jeremy, fearful lest a meeting should bring an unendurable vividness to his memories. But one autumn day, deciding to bite the bullet, he put pen to paper. Jeremy replied effusively and expressed genuine delight at having word from George after all these years.

Later that month, George and "Jerry" spent a happy day together at Kew. Their old friendship rekindled immediately and they shared cheerful memories. Jeremy was very sad that he'd lost contact with Alice and still more disappointed that George brought no news of her. It was October 29th, 1957 and the gardens were not at the height of colour, but George had chosen the day deliberately. Wherever she was, if she was still living, it was Alice's seventieth birthday.

28

Thursday December 30th, 1965 – Saturday January 1st, 1966

The journey was an awkward one. George booked a ticket on an afternoon train from Truro, arriving in Paddington shortly after 9pm. He would overnight in London at a hotel near Kings Cross Station and travel onwards to Whitby the next day, leaving at noon, changing trains at Darlington and Middlesbrough before arriving at his destination at 7.30pm. Rose rang at the time appointed and they agreed to meet at Whitby railway station.

The atmosphere in Boulby Cliff House on the Friday was charged with something for which Rose had no name, and the prospect of reunion that evening produced an increased mobility in Alice. Rose found her wandering around the house, gazing out of the windows, fidgeting, lifting and inspecting ornaments in which she'd exhibited no previous interest. Alice made several visits to the potting shed and to the cliff edge. Rose's own pulse was raised in excitement, and on more than one occasion she found herself muttering under her breath, "Calm down, calm down…" both on her own behalf and for Alice.

The time approached. Rose reached out and brought Alice to a halt.

"Alice." Alice looked at her and Rose saw that her eyes were wide with anticipation and excitement. Her breathing was a little accelerated and her chest visibly rose and fell. "Alice, I'm going to Whitby now – to meet George. I'll be back soon my love."

Rose walked to the main road and took the bus to Whitby, arriving about half an hour early. She sat in the station café, drank tea and watched the minutes tick by on the clock.

In due course George's train pulled in. Rose found herself almost unable to stand. Her heart was racing, and she was so excited she thought she might burst. Standing on the platform Rose suddenly realised she had little idea what George looked like, having seen him before only in his wedding photographs taken fifty-five years earlier. Mercifully the train wasn't full and she was able to guess that the tall man carrying a small suitcase, clearly looking out for someone, must be him.

"Rose?" he said, approaching her.

"George!" She almost burst into tears, and hugged him.

"Oh my goodness. That welcome was worth the journey," he said when she let him go.

She took his suitcase from him. It wasn't heavy. "Come and have a cuppa. We have to talk."

They found a quiet corner of the café and Rose ordered another pot of tea.

She was sitting opposite him. There was no point in beating about the bush.

"George," she said, looking directly at him. "Alice is here."

"*What?*" Now it was his turn to break down. He buried his face in his hands and his shoulders shook with emotion for several moments. A few of the other customers looked over but Rose, her own eyes wet, gently waved at them, indicating that all was okay. Eventually George regained control. Raising his head and wiping his cheeks he said, "How?"

"I can't tell you that George."

"But is she all right? Where has she been all these years? Why come back now?"

"It isn't easy to answer all those questions, but let me try. Is she all right? Yes, I think so. Where has she been all these years? I could give you a very precise answer to that question, but I think I'd better not – at least not yet. Why come back now? That's the easy one. Because of *you* George! Because of *you!*"

"Can I see her?"

"Yes, let's go." She'd begun to rise but sat quickly down again.

"George, look at me." He did so, and she took both his hands in hers, squeezing them gently. "You're going to get the biggest shock of your life tonight." He was looking intently at her. "Everything you thought was real, everything you thought was normal... you'll have to let go of it all."

George looked puzzled. He knit his brow. "...what do you mean...?"

She said, quietly and deliberately, "This world, the past, the future, what you think you know, everything you thought you *ever* knew. You'll need to set it all aside. Tonight. Here and now. Please don't think I'm exaggerating."

"I'll do anything. I just want to see Alice."

Eyes, penetrating into his soul: "Do you understand me George?"

George felt strangely off centre. Rose had led him into a new place. He felt an unusual calmness.

"I do."

They took a taxi to the house and Rose opened the front door as the car pulled away. George looked about him as he walked along the front path. The fruit trees were much larger now, the old vegetable beds appeared much the same. After all these years he was back. He'd never expected to see this house again. Rose beckoned him in. She put his suitcase down and took his hat and coat, hanging them up by the staircase. Then she turned back to him, looked into his eyes silently, and smiled.

Then she opened the sitting room door.

He walked in.

The electric light was on. Alice was standing in the middle of the room. George had prepared himself to meet an elderly woman of seventy-eight, but the person before him was the Alice he remembered – the beautiful, brown-haired girl of twenty-seven he'd held in his memory for fifty years. His mouth dropped open and he cupped the sides of his head with his hands, unable to speak.

She held out her hands. "Hello George," said Alice. "Welcome home."

Rose, watching from the doorway, felt the emotion catch in her chest and tears sprung from her eyes.

George walked towards Alice. He sobbed uncontrollably. "I'm so sorry, I'm so sorry, Alice."

Rose stood there long enough to see the two of them enfolded in each other's arms. Then she said quietly, "I'll leave you two alone. Have a lovely evening. See you in the morning." Then she withdrew to the television room and switched on the set. As midnight approached she poured herself her annual glass of sherry and saw in the New Year with Andy Stewart at *The White Heather Club*.

Half an hour after midnight Rose emerged from the TV room and crept downstairs. The house was in darkness. The sitting room and kitchen were unoccupied and both front and back doors were locked. George's hat and coat were still hanging up but his suitcase was gone. Creeping back upstairs, she saw that the door to the second bedroom was closed.

The house was silent.

In the morning Rose woke late – as she always did after a glass of sherry. It was almost nine o'clock. As she crossed the landing she looked over at the spare bedroom and saw that the door was standing open. Peering in she could see that the bed had been stripped, bedclothes and pillowcases piled at its foot. The morning light streamed into the bathroom and Rose opened the window to commence her morning toilette. The sun had risen just a little higher than the cliff edge and its light glared directly into her eyes. But, squinting against it, she could just make out the figures of Alice and George embracing at the end of the garden. There was something different. Rose couldn't see very clearly against the brilliant sunlight, but it seemed to her that George appeared, somehow, younger.

Rose spent a few minutes in the bathroom, then dressed herself. As she made her way downstairs she heard someone singing – a slow, sustained melody, wordless and ecstatic. It was so hauntingly beautiful that she stood motionless, listening for some time. As it faded she noticed that George's hat and coat had gone.

Alice was waiting for her in the kitchen and gave her a huge hug when she appeared.

"Where's George?" asked Rose.

Alice replied, "George has gone on ahead."

Rose's instincts told her not to inquire further.

"I love you Rose," said Alice. "Never forget. I'll always be close to you."

Rose kissed her on the forehead as she had before. The gesture felt very natural. Alice felt like a daughter to her.

Rose smiled and said, "I'll put the kettle on."

She turned and began to make tea. As she stood at the sink, looking out at the garden, bathed in the morning light shining through the window, she knew that Alice was gone.

Rose was alone in the kitchen.

The circle was closed.

EPILOGUE

Rose

Rose lived on at Boulby Cliff House alone, although she still had the company of her twelve books, her television and her tape recorder. She did occasionally visit Jimmy and Jenny Jackson and made a handful of new friends. Rose's association with Alice had changed her in some ways and she found herself less awkward in the company of others.

She had a telephone installed in 1972. Rose had tried to call George several times in the days following his visit but there was never any reply, and a year later she found that his number was no longer in use.

She kept up her intermittent tape recordings, sending messages to Agnes. Rose would tell her about Alice, George, Jimmy and Jenny. Again and again she shared with her mother her perpetual ineptness in the kitchen. She grew a few fruits and vegetables in the garden but was content to let most of it run wild.

A year or so after Alice, Rose took in a stray dog and named him George. George kept her company for nearly ten years, and when he died Rose found herself so upset that she decided not to keep another. Time was taking everything.

The people she knew gradually disappeared. First Tommy retired, then Jenny died, Jimmy following not long after. The years and the decades closed in and Rose sometimes wondered if any of it had really happened. She lost another fifteen feet of garden to the sea. The earth bed that had enclosed Alice's grave tumbled over the edge and added to the scree below. Rose often stood at the eastern end of the garden as she had with Alice the day that George's letters had arrived, a lone ageing figure, her gaze following the North Sea to the furthest limit of visibility while her mind scanned the horizon of her memory. Her eyes dimmed and her frame became ever more frail and bent.

Rose became increasingly infirm, and fell from time to time. She had to call the doctor on more than one occasion and he suggested that she move into a nursing home. Rose resisted for several years, but after a particularly nasty tumble down the stairs tearfully gave in. She moved out of Boulby Cliff House and into the Esk Valley Nursing Home in May 1997. It was a wrench. She'd spent seventy-four years of her life in the house.

Rose lived on in the nursing home. She became friendly with some of the other residents but never received visitors from the world outside. There was no one left who knew her. Time slipped away like sand through the fingers…

Tuesday December 8th, 2015

Rose is 101 years old. She is very frail and sits alone, a blanket covering her lap. Her vision is limited and she can no longer read. Although she cannot see the TV screen very well Rose still looks forward to *Doctor Who*. *Hell Bent*, with Peter Capaldi is still fresh in her mind from three days ago.

It is four o'clock and Rose is very tired. She hears footsteps approaching. Rose has learned each staff member by heart. She knows which nurse is coming just by the sound of their shoes, the way they walk. But the footsteps she hears now are new. Rose looks up. Someone is coming. She sees the blue floral dress, the brown hair…

Wednesday December 9th, 2015

Diane and Bridget, two nurses at the Esk Valley Nursing Home:

Diane: Sad news about Rose. She was a lovely lady.
Bridget: Aye she was. She had a very good innings though.
Diane: Too early to know about the funeral I s'pose?
Bridget: Aye. Next week probably.
Diane: Sad. All alone, for all those years.
Bridget: Very sad… Weird yesterday though.
Diane: Why's that?

Bridget: She had a visitor.
Diane: Rose *never* had visitors!
Bridget: Claimed to be an old friend of hers. Young woman. Nicely turned out. Blue flowery dress. Sat with her for hours. I've never seen Rose so happy.

ABOUT THE AUTHOR

Kevin Corby Bowyer was born in Southend-on-Sea in 1961. He spent most of his life as a professional musician, travelling the world, playing solo concerts, making commercial recordings and trying to teach others how to play. He always thought about his musical performances as acts of storytelling.

The tale of Rose, Alice and George spent years tumbling around in his head, and now he's had the time to spin it.

Kevin lives in Scotland. He worries too much and considers himself too old for most things.

Kevin Bowyer (photo: Tommy Ga Ken Wan)

ACKNOWLEDGEMENTS

My wife Sandra is a keen gardener. One day she dug up a suspicious-looking old shower curtain. It didn't have a body inside but it did set my mind in motion. So thanks to her for that. Thanks also to whoever it was who buried the shower curtain.

My proof readers did an amazing job. So thanks to:

1. My daughter, Jeanne Loganbill, a seasoned professional writer, who put in hours of suggestions and taught me a lot about the craft.

2. Another daughter, Nadia Humphreys, a professional Yorkshire gal, who corrected all my Yorkshire dialect.

3. Sandra, who offered many suggestions, designed the Boulby Cliff House garden and pointed out a few bits of clumsy stage management.

4. Thanks also to Elspeth Johnstone, who read through the text carefully and actually said she enjoyed it.

5. And thanks to Joseph Loganbill, who created the magnificent cover. You can view more of Joe's amazing work here: www.josephloganbill.com

Thanks to you for taking the time to read.

And thanks to Rose, who grew in my head but who now seems almost as real to me as anyone else does.

Printed in Great Britain
by Amazon